Muted Echoes

Joe Bliskey

ISBN: 978-0-9960592-0-6
Different Drum Books

DEDICATION

To Courtney and Chelsa.

CONTENTS

ACKNOWLEDGMENTS

I am deeply indebted to my wife, Etta for her patience,
support and literary advice.

Thanks also to Paul Dietz for his hours of editing and his kindness.

Special thanks to Phil Anstrom for his expert coaching while
getting the chinks out of my armor.

Cover Art by Susannah Blanton

Layout by Tracy Peel.

1

RIVER OF PAIN

Karl Lundquist died in the Clarion River in the Spring of 1941. His grandson Karl Daugherty discovered his body in a fishing hole in Johnsonburg Pennsylvania.

The Lundquists lived on Venors Island, not an island at all, but a finger of land pointing into the river that the French and the Indians called the River of Pain. It had been a bloody place not far from the Seneca Tribe's regular wide but shallow ford. The Daughertys lived near that river too, about six miles to the south in Ridgeway.

Karl Daugherty was fair-haired and jovial. He had a wisp of straight blond hair in front that would cluster in curls under his hat brim. He had eyes that would cut steel and yet when he looked at you they gleamed. Blue eyes looked out from a deep brow, almost too deep. His habit was to shake his head and laugh in a quiet burst about nearly everything. This made him seem the simpleton at times with the rubbing of his chin and his ffuh-huh giggle. But Karl would often shock people who didn't know him with a great quip or a profundity. His bluntness was stark yet respectful and gentle. He often showed a wisdom beyond his years. When he went to his grandfather's funeral he tried to help Eunice keep things light, tried to buoy his sister up. But after the burial he became solemn, mournful and still.

After the funeral Eunice and Karl caught a ride from their cousin Eric who dropped them off still dressed in their Sunday clothes at the scene of their grandfather's drowning. Eunice stood near the bank and wind rustled the treetops and reduced her careful hairdo to a mop. She had her back to her brother who told her what happened that day.

"We were on the river about an hour and Grandpa sent me off to collect a handful of grasshoppers for bait. He caught a small brown trout, barely legal. He cut him open and saw what they were feeding on. They weren't too interested in our salted minnows."

"I was getting impatient trying to scoop grasshoppers up with my hands. After about twenty minutes all I had was two or three of them in my creel. I put a clump of ferns over the hole in the basket to keep them from jumping out. I was in a rush, all the time worried about missing the action while Grandpa fished the river. I thought he could fish everything out of every hole before I got back. I guess I forgot they weren't hitting on minnows. "Go catch us some grasshoppers, Karly," he said, "and I'll fool around in this hole with these minnas a while and see if I can't raise something."

"Yeah, Karly," Eunice said, "he was the only one who could get away with calling you that. He could do no wrong."

"That's right. And he never said a cross word about a soul. He had a soft spot in his heart for you too."

"I know it." Eunice saw the woods blur before her then come back into focus when the tears splashed her good dress.

Karl went back to his story. "I was determined not to get stumped that morning. Grandpa called it getting skunked. He already had one and I had nothing. I thought we could catch plenty of trout but first I needed at least a dozen more grasshoppers. The river was slow and wide there. I was in a sunken bog about forty yards south of here. Grandpa was directly behind me but concealed by that ridge with all the brush on it. Some of the bushes were thick with blossoms. The dump is over that way." Karl pointed across the river and to the south. "The wind was coming out of the northeast so I couldn't smell the rot of it. That wind was blowing just like it is now, with authority through the hollow, hard enough to rustle the berry bushes." Karl and Eunice both stared for a minute down the hollow, traced by a dirt road bed that swooped toward the bog and had some big pine logs serving as guard rails on the sharp bend dead east of them. You could see those logs clearly, awash in sunlight and studded with pale spots where their branches used to be. "I was looking over at those logs at the edge of that road there while I was picking more ferns for my creel. I flushed a half-dozen grasshoppers out of the ferns when I heard an engine start on the dirt road up there. I heard tires popping on rock and some booming sounds like something banging around in the back of a truck. When I looked up at the road I saw a green truck with a white roof on it. I could see the diesel smoke, and I could hear the engine sound falling off and echoing through the hollow. And then it grew faint and finally out of range."

"When I got back here with the grasshoppers, grandpa's rod and a tinfoil pouch of minnows were on the ground like he'd thrown them there. That's something he would never, ever do. The brass reel cover was gashed on one side, knocked crooked and all smeared up with mud. I was yelling for him. I'm telling you Eunie, something about that day was all wrong. I just can't put it together."

"Don't worry yourself with all of that, Karl. It's done now. I know how you feel, like you should have done something. But what could you have done? Try to put it behind you now. Remember the good things."

The Elk County Coroner's report said that Karl Lundquist had a heart attack and slipped into the current or perhaps he had fallen into a deep hole and filled his waders and couldn't get out. For Karl, who never believed the coroner, and couldn't put it behind him, that day had marked him. He often had the same maddeningly remorseful dreams of a thousand different versions of what happened that afternoon. All of them included Karl's intervention and ended with a hike with grandpa back to his place stride for stride in their muddy fishing boots.

That day at breakfast, Connor Daugherty told his son to put those things out of his mind. Eunice was sitting across the table from Connor and he talked past her to Karl who was behind her making his toast. He told the boy that his father-in-law was an expert fisherman and smart about the woods, trout streams and rivers. "He looked as healthy as a draft horse and he'd never be reckless or do anything stupid. You can't control fate. He must've had a bad heart all the time and never knew it." *Anyting*, he had said, and Eunice cringed like she always did when her father's accent stuck out like that. Karl saw her do it and scowled quickly in response. He had heard her complaints about the old world manner of speaking. She would never mention it to her parents.

Eunice was peculiar when it came to her idea of American. She listened to the radio dramas with characters slinging their slang and popping fingers to jazz tunes. She had seen *The Shop Around the Corner* and *Pinocchio* at the Strand Theatre. Stories with characters who were so foreign, like the woodcarver who made the marionette and the old shop keeper with his heavy Hungarian accent. The young store clerks were so sharp looking and polished but they talked like people she knew (or maybe kids in Ridgway worked hard to sound like them). The cartoon woodcarver seemed so anachronistic compared to the puppet who spoke like a new-world child.

She would see old men like Tony Patotti in town tip their hats and greet her mother and dad in their broken English. Patotti was nearly always soiled and grimy with his old stake truck and coveralls smelling of oil. There was a young swell with him one morning at the train station. He looked out of place, mid to late twenties and not typical company for Patotti. They talked to her father for a few minutes and both left in ragged, muddy trucks. The younger one spoke with a different accent, not Irish or British but similar and his clothing was like a young man on a fox hunt. He wore expensive riding boots and corduroy jacket with a suede

4

cut-out on the shoulder. Though there was mud splashed on his fenders and behind his iron bumpers, there was none on his clothes or boots. His truck clattered and belched acrid black diesel smoke. It was green and white with a simple diamond trade mark on its door with lettering around it: Yates Well Supply, Dubois. He crossed the tracks and two large steel drums boomed from the bed behind him. He drove north toward Johnsonburg and Eunice never gave the man another thought until her brother mentioned the truck on the road near the Clarion River. "It's done now." That's what she said to Karl. It was not unusual to see a green pickup out in the wild places of Elk County. There were probably a few dozen green trucks banging around in these woods. Forestry trucks, loggers, guys working on gas wells, which were ubiquitous. She kept silent about it.

2

DRIED FLOWERS AND SHOTGUN SHELLS

Thanksgiving morning, the Daugherty house was arranged like a homely dime store print of a family holiday, composed and overlaid with soft blends of color, a portrait nearly escaping the darkness behind them. The pot belly stove was finally doing its job but Eunice had on an extra sweater which made her movements clumsy as she chose three rugged, heavy logs from the porch stack. She crooked a fourth one in her neck where it threatened to tumble and it pricked and pinched there and turned her skin crimson and dotted with near-bloody spots. There was a shotgun report from across the ridge. It had a whole different sound from one you would hear in the Summer, kind of a dull reverberation that owes its softness to its travel over a blanket of snow. A chunk of snow detached from the apple tree on the edge of the property as if knocked off by the sound. It dropped straight down and disappeared in the whiteness. Eunice watched it fall with indifference, too loaded down with firewood to shrug. She laid the fuel into the scuttle on top of its remaining chunky black jewels and took her seat at the table with a blue and white saucer of roasted chestnuts and a copy of Mrs. Miniver. The book lay where she had left it with a letter opener holding her place. She dog-eared her page and, with the paper knife, pried the hull off of a nut, biting in to find it was spoiled. The others had tasted fine, still soft and warm from the stovetop. She spit the chewed up pulp into a napkin and leaned back against her chair back with a creak. Her father's head jerked back and forth ever so slightly.

Over her dad's shoulder Eunice could see a copy of the town newspaper, The Ridgway Record. From Eunice's perspective, her father, Connor was rimmed in a bright aura from the glare of the morning sun bounding off of a foot of overnight snow. She pushed some remnant chestnut pieces, bitter and mushy, to the back of her front teeth and spit the brown flecks to the floor. She darted a quick glance at her mother to be sure she hadn't seen or heard her spit. Too unladylike. Her mom, engrossed in meal preparations, never flinched. Her dad's bald spot looked so large now on the back of his head. The lamp by the couch brought the shine out of it as he read the news. She looked for a while at his fine, black hair on the borders of his baldness. He always looked so strong and handsome to Eunice. Now he had this empty patch contrasting his dark hair that was like a trimmed-out wooded place. She wanted to put his ball cap over it. He wasn't that old. He had none of the feebleness of the old men she knew, none of their old man smell and no sign of their careless forgetfulness, stains of tobacco spit on the sides of their mouths, and patched-up shirts that hang too loosely on their bones.

Verna, Eunice's mom was in the kitchen rattling pans and measuring cups about in the industry of a holiday meal. She would be putting together some pies, pecan and pumpkin. Eunice looked over at her as she brought down a wide-bladed knife on a pile of shelled nuts in such expert, rapid chopping. In a few minutes Eunice would shut her book with a happy thud and help knead and roll out dough on wax paper dusted with flour. A younger Eunice much preferred reading to helping in the kitchen. Her mother encouraged her children to embrace literacy. She bought them each a best-selling work of fiction as a birthday gift. It would always be published the same year of that birthday. Eunice sat at this same table religiously each holiday with whatever book she received that year, or if she had finished it before Thanksgiving, she would read Karl's birthday book. This year was different because Eunice had grown out of her juvenile game of faking deep interest in the read then protesting vigorously when called to the kitchen. "But Mom," she would say with great dramatic flourish, "I'm enriching my mind just now." She was sixteen now. Helping out gave Eunice a kick. Verna got a little time to sit down and just chat.

It did not seem like Thanksgiving without a big, steamy, brown turkey in a roasting pan with stuffing busting out of it. Eunice closed her eyes and recalled a picture of a roasted bird in the Look Magazine she read at the hairdresser's. They were having pheasant instead. Connor had shot the bird at the Airport. There were no airplanes there, just an unpaved strip on top of a hill where they occasionally landed a few small planes. The Army Air Corps were prepared to put a few recon planes and fighters up there if the need ever came, as if the Japs or the Germans would ever give a hoot about this place. Nothing here could possibly interest them. Trees, a few ugly furniture factories, a plugged-up courthouse cannon and a place where they make ink. The bits of chestnut still in her mouth triggered her memory. The sensation took her back to last Fall when her Uncle Sean came by for their game feast.

Eunice had taken a fork full of rabbit and nearly broke a molar on a piece of birdshot which she had spit out with such vigor that it ricocheted off the gravy boat. Her mother was appalled, not because Eunice had nearly swallowed a lead pellet, but because she had launched it like from a slingshot at the dinner table. Uncle Sean laughed and stomped the floor until Verna's china clinked behind him in the hutch. He said, "Eunie, I'll have my dogs trained by next season and you can hunt pheasant with me. I'll let you clean the birds. You'll have an eye for the loose bb's. I'm pretty sure!" Dad, restraining his laughter with a stern clearing of the throat that disguised nothing, said, "We'll make it a threesome. That is, if you want to, Eunice."

Eunice had learned to shoot five years ago at age eleven and she was a pretty fair hand with the clay pigeons. Her first shot stamped her right cheek because she didn't shoulder it right but, since the blood was minimal and no teeth were loose, she didn't quit. When Verna saw that bruise she said immediately that it might be the wrong kind of pursuit for a girl. She was looking straight at Connor when she said it. Her brother Karl loved to hunt small game and deer but he could never get the knack for shooting things out of the air. He was a year older than Eunice and had learned to shoot when he was nine. When their Uncle Sean made his offer, Karl and everyone else understood why the invitation was for a threesome and not a hunting quartet. There were no hard feelings. Karl would be busy building his two-way radio anyway.

It was 1942. Eunice Daugherty was growing into a solid wholesomeness. Maybe into a beauty in the girl-next-door sort of way but next door was nearly a mile to the north.

As that year passed there was plenty of preparation. They had made a number of dry runs to the dog training area by Little Mill Creek. She worked on her shooting some more and on her first hunt she bagged two pheasant and a grouse. That day when Eunice came home with her three birds Karl said, "You're amazing. How did I get a sis like you!" She said, "I don't know, but there isn't a thing I can do about it." Karl put her in a headlock and twisted an ear. "Meet me tomorrow on the tennis court. I'll do somethin' about it."

They wrestled around on the living room floor. Eunice was sweating in her wool hunting pants. Connor came in after he cleaned his gun out on the porch. He entered without a word, carrying his shotgun like it weighed a hundred pounds and leaned it in the corner. Karl said, "Any luck today Dad? You're back awful soon."

"Nope. Now that'll be enough of your rough housing. Go do something constructive." Eunice got Mrs. Miniver down from the shelf and pretended to read.

"Eunice. Clean your gun."

As she ran the ramrod down the barrel of the twelve gauge Eunice mumbled about her father's cantankerous mood. She was shoving the oil rag with a little too much vigor. Connor said, "Go easy there, Eunice, mind the firing pin." Why should he take things out on her? They had had a tense ride home from the woods. Connor and Sean got into an argument. Connor said, "If you liked the hunting better in Armaugh why didn't you stay there?

And what became of your murderin' friends back home? The ones hunting people? That fine boy, Stephen Hayes, so handy he was with a pack of cards and a pistol, where's he been keeping himself?"

Eunice could not make out the source of their ire. She was moving from shelter to shelter in her mind to escape a storm of oppressive confusion. Verna said she was no more or less confused than anyone else her age and, in many ways, she was way ahead of the other girls. If Verna was right about that, Eunice didn't see it. They argued that morning. Arguments with Verna went nowhere. Especially when Eunice, with no apparent logic, insisted on returning to her old complaint again and again: Why did they have to live so far from town?

Her old diary, now a pile of ashes long gone, had a short lament in it. It said:

> Will I ever understand the fuss
> Over boys and how they're not like us?
> And do I try to be the friend
> Of every smart looking girl
> Just so I can get close
> To the smart looking boys?
> How will I ever know
> How to talk to a beau?
> How will I ever know how to act
> Watching foxes snoop around our barn
> Way up here in this mountainous wilderness?

While her father and uncle had their tiff Eunice was lost in her own little world. Still puzzled. Still mired in the shadowy loneliness that struck her so often on that hilltop. When it came over her it was nearly physical. It was the opposite of the palpable stirring she felt when Kevin Barry came to visit Karl. When Kevin was in their house she got all worked up with odd feelings she had no idea what to do with. Arguing with Verna left her with those regrets you get when you should have said this or done that. Verna told her, "Learn to bloom where you're planted." So she went about, often in a funk, trying to work out what the hell that meant, collecting dried flowers and shotgun shells for reloading, and storing them together under her bed in the box her father's work boots had come in.

3

SERVING PRACTICE AND SERVING
PHEASANT

Karl loved the game of tennis. Even a foot of snow couldn't keep him from his dedicated practice. Nobody played much tennis in Ridgway in 1942. Baseball, basketball and football yes, but tennis was for the country club set. That was what Connor told Karl. "Since late in the last century tennis was played in the royal European courts and on some rich bastard's croquet lawn. A prince's game. Over here it tends to be the pastime of the doctor's and lawyer's kids." The subject of the aristocratic roots of tennis came up when Karl said he wanted a job helping the country club's groundskeeper so he could use the only tennis courts in town. Ignoring Connor's kindly steerage of his boy back to his social station, Karl persisted. Connor said, "Go out there and see a guy named Archie Mahoney. Tell him what you're about." Karl read a defeated finality in his father's voice, as if the trip out to the rolling green lawns of the Ridgway Country Club would just be for naught.

The next morning early, Karl took his bike out to see Mahoney. It would be his first conversation with him. He knew the groundskeeper only as a dull guy with dirt on his pants who spoke in a monotone. Sure, he had seen him around town but the

Mahoneys went to the Catholic church and the kids went to Saint Leo's. Archie droned at him that morning, "Listen son, you are either too dumb to know that I don't exactly get along with your old man and I never will, either, or..." he spat a stream of tobacco juice on a peony bush, a brown jet that washed three or four ants off of it, "...or you got the biggest balls in town." Karl squinted one eye a little for effect and rubbed at his chin. He was calm and measured as he came back at Mahoney without hesitation or rancor. "Respectfully, sir, I'm not my daddy and I want to work here. You have an opening and I have the muscle and sweat required to help you make this place look good. I'll work the first week free and you tell me on Friday whether my balls and all my other parts are big enough. Can I work here a week, Mister Mahoney?"

Karl got his job and his access to the tennis courts. He was paid for his first week at the club. Spring through late Fall he was out there until darkness sent him home. In the Summer he'd burn his lunch breaks hitting balls. If the courts were occupied he'd take on winners. By July he began to show his skills and his serve was already blazing and accurate. Not everyone would play with him after he began to shine on the court. It wouldn't do for some of the more spineless players to take a drubbing from that Daugherty boy with the patches on his pants. Karl's new found talent became his favorite obsession.

Now in the November cold he was on the court again hitting buckets of tennis balls. He was out there that Thanksgiving morning with his snow shovel. He had promised to be home by noon.

The other Daughertys were snug in their house on the hill. The smells from the kitchen made some delicious promises they knew would be kept very soon. At 11 A. M. a loud pounding issued from the big oak front door. Connor folded the newspaper and put it down. He adjusted his reading glasses farther downward on his nose so he could peer over them at the door. As he did, the banging got louder and longer. "That has to be Uncle Sean," Eunice said. Connor glanced across his flannel shoulder and gave a quick wink over his glasses. Still looking in her direction, he called out, "Who's doing all that pounding? You're not a peddler are you? We don't like peddlers up here." Eunice laughed out loud and hammered at her knees. The answer came half muffled, then clearly once the door swung open. It swung out wide until it struck the doorstop and bounced back shuddering. Sean stopped it with a foot, his hands occupied with a nail keg. Verna had a hand on her hip as she pushed a damp curl straightening itself out above her eye. This left a ghostly swipe of flour on her forehead. She looked back and forth between the brothers, eager for the next bit of banter and waiting for her chance to say what anyone in the family could predict she would, "Alright boys, simmer." Between alright and boys came another banging from the dining room table where Sean was pulling jars and cans out of the little barrel. Holding each of them up for examination as if his eyes were bad, "That wouldn't be it. Nope, not that." He set a cranberry sauce and a marmalade jar and the sack of sugar in a semi-circle around the wooden keg. Connor said, "So who told you to bring half of the damn market up here, then?" Sean kept on with his inventory and didn't acknowledge his brother. He held a big Hershey bar up to the light, "That for sure is not it. How'd that get in there? Never touch the stuff," he said as he sailed it into his niece's hands. "It's gigantic!" she said, "like the ones at the movie theatre. Thank you, Uncle Sean. You're the best." Sean gave her a backhanded wave and a dismissive growl. He reached into the keg again and drew out a pint of Bushmills, "Ah, I knew I packed the cough medicine. Catching cold, I am." He kissed the bottle before tossing it to his brother. He pulled a yellow fishing knife out too with a red ribbon tied to it. "What's this, early Christmas?" asked Connor.

"It's yours, Connor. Fell out of my jacket on my closet floor. I found it this morning. I borrowed it up at Little Mill Creek that day I had that creel full of big brookies to clean and you had your two bitty minnows already gutted. Remember that, Connor?"

"Yeah, your near constant reminders are helpful, Seanny. Very helpful with my old, feeble memory and all. But you are the one feeble in your head, gift wrapping my own knife like that."

"Returning your goods is the Christian thing to do. I've reformed. God was sending me a sign dropping it on my closet floor. I'm keenly aware of the spiritual these days."

Verna handed her apron over to Eunice and took a seat next to the dining room table. Eunice was walking straight to the big ball of dough that awaited her. Verna said, "This is a day for giving thanks, Sean. You shouldn't be so flip about these things." She was looking at Eunice's back as she said it. Sean snatched the red plaid hunting hat off his head and held it meekly in front of him. "Of course. You're right Verna, and I meant no disrespect." Connor had just uncorked the pint of Bushmills and taken himself a healthy haul. With his voice box pinched by the burn of it he said, "Yeah Sean, show some goddamn reverence." Eunice, bursting forth with a laugh she couldn't contain, blew a cloud of flour off the kitchen counter. The rest all joined her at once, even Verna who had her head in her hands as if she were contemplating what to do with the menfolk. The laughing stopped abruptly when the front door opened again and a gust of chill wind blew frozen maple leaves onto the linoleum. Karl came in crunching on the leaves with an ugly cut on his eyebrow. He flung his broken tennis racket aside. It rested forlornly on the sofa with the top half of its netting drooping over the arm. Verna got a cold, damp cloth and put it on his eye. Karl looked around with his good eye and held the compress on the other. "I got a couple of licks in," he said, as if it would be hard for them to believe. His mother said, "I'm sure you did but who broke your eye and what happened to that racket you saved up to buy for over a month?"

"Got busted."

"I see that," Verna said as she turned his face so his clear eye could see that she wanted more of an answer. "What happened son?" Connor asked. Sean and Eunice looked on from beside the nail keg.

"Do I have to?"

"Well sure you do, Karl. Go on."

"I don't want to wreck our dinner."

"Don't be worrying about that. Now what happened? Were you at the country club?"

"Yeah. I was working on my serve. I had just got everything shoveled off. Here comes Mickey Mahoney with a quart of Rolling Rock in a paper bag. He was pretty well schnockered."

Mickey Mahoney, Archie's twenty year old son came around the club to help out on some busy Spring weekends. He and Karl had tangled before. He wore white undershirts and slicked his hair down. He had a pointed-looking nose and dark eyebrows that sat high and made him look like he was constantly considering an insult. He liked to sneer at Karl and kept calling him boy. "Go get me a rake out of the shed, boy." One August afternoon Mickey came to ask Archie for money for some beer to take out to Sandy Beach. He had two fingers taped and splinted. He held them up in Karl's face and said, "See this, Karly boy? Your dirty-fighting uncle did this. He thinks he's tough shit." Karl tilted his head slightly to emphasize his inspection of some fresh, pinkness of healing. "Well," said Karl, "you're the guy with the cauliflower ear and the crippled hand. My uncle looks fresh as a daisy." Mickey shoved Karl, who stood his ground. "I wouldn't go shoving people."

"Who's gonna stop me? You? Well you better bring a lunch. I'm going to get Sean Daugherty, though. Write it down." Mickey was huffing like a train and turned to rush off.

"Write it down? Ok. But I don't know how to spell Mickey's annihilation."

Mickey turned around, but stopped abruptly. His shoe rasped on the gravel under it. Archie was returning from the office with some folding money in his hand. Karl continued spreading manure in a bed of pansies as though none of Mickey's posturing and threatening mattered. "Funny man," Mickey said and got in his beat-up Buick, with its rotted fenders and flat paint, squealing tires into a fishtail and nearly hitting the gate. Everyone in town knew that car. Some avoided the places they saw it parked.

Mickey's personal war with the Daughertys had begun two days before that summer afternoon at the country club. There was a serious set-to between Sean and Mickey that had occurred at Twin Lakes where they were both on a crew building log buildings for the State Parks Commission. A Brownie troop was there for a swimming party and Eunice was among the chaperones. Sean was sitting at a picnic table no more than 15 feet away unwrapping a sandwich in waxed paper. Mickey turned to a young co-worker named Francis Degastino and said, "Hey, Meatball that's a real cute one there. Soon as she gets some titties, I'm fuckin' her. Putting my dibs in now." Francis was looking straight ahead and half-finished saying, "She's a little kid, Mickey."

"Well, how about the Daugherty girl. She looks ready to go to me."

"You're not funny, Mahoney," said Francis. Francis turned his back to gather the remains of his lunch to go off by himself. He muttered, "And quit calling me Meatball." He heard a scuffle developing behind him.

Sean had lifted Mickey completely off the ground and dangled him by his throat. Mickey was choking and prying at Sean's arm. He managed to say, "Let me have some air, will you?"

"I'll give you enough air to take that back." Sean set Mickey back on his feet. That's my niece you are drooling over and Francis is right. That other girl is practically a baby, and you are an insufferable asshole who needs to apologize. I will accept your public and heartfelt contrition on my niece's behalf. You'll not touch her or mention her name again where I can hear it."

Mickey made his second mistake that afternoon by poking his index and middle fingers into Sean Daugherty's unyielding left pectoral muscle and saying, "I don't take shit back and I fuck whoever I want to. This is America." In a flash, Sean had a handful of those stabbing fingers. You could hear the cracking of Mickey's two digits. He cried out, "You bastard, that's not clean fighting," he began to sob. Sean instantly battered him with four blows, two on each side of his oily head and Mahoney went down clutching at his ears. He held up the two sore fingers like pantomime Indian feathers in a sad charade on the ground. Sean said, "That clean enough?" He wasn't even breathing hard and he betrayed no agitation. When a park ranger rushed to break up the fight it was already over. "Recess is over, kids. No more of that or you're both fired. Get back to work," he said. Sean would have no trouble with Mickey Mahoney the rest of the summer but he never showed him his back, either.

Mickey would scheme and plan throughout the entire year for a way to get back at Sean. Until he could work out his plan, Karl would have to be a suitable proxy for his wrath. On Thanksgiving morning Mickey had an early start on his beer and was looking hunched and clenched up. Kicking at the snow as he walked. Muttering to himself. He had been wandering around the country club grounds alone and had talked to almost nobody except Archie all day.

Mickey's father had dispatched him with disgust and anger from the breakfast table just after dawn. It was about charges that were formally filed against his son. Mickey wandered and brooded about the story that would be presented at his hearing, a story about a sixteen year old girl and what the police report said happened to her in a storage area behind the stage at the high school auditorium. The girl was Kathleen Dozier. She was getting dressed for her part in a play when he just forced his way into the store room and attacked her.

Archie Mahoney told Mickey to mark down the court date that morning and he said that this was not the small matter Mickey insisted it was. Just kid stuff, fooling around a little. "No Mickey, guys do jail time for this kind of shit. A child, Mickey! A sixteen year old honor student. Not a retarded girl like the last one. You said you learned your lesson and her folks let it go." Archie smacked his son's face hard enough to make his ears ring but Mickey heard his father's message clearly enough. "You got real trouble now boy and you're gonna take your lumps. There's nothing I can do this time, even if I wanted to."

The lurid tale was all over town. She was a pretty, blonde-haired, blue-eyed cheerleader and a candy striper at Elk County

General. Witnesses had heard her screaming, "No, get away from me, Mickey!" Her father, an attorney, was going for the jugular, of course. Minutes before he arrived at the country club parking lot Mickey had been talking to one of his drinking buddies, Speck Robinson. Spec was behind the A and P shoveling snow. He paused for a sip of beer with him. Mickey vented, saying that the girl's father was just being unreasonable. The judge was out to get him and his own father was too mean or too lazy to back him up. "I'm going to have to say that little cheerleader lured me into that store room, flirting with me, reaching for me." Now he marched himself through the snow mumbling, "The jury would understand, she egged me on... unless they're just as mean and unreasonable as everyone else." Mickey planted a step too forcefully. His boot slid ahead of him pushing up the icy top layer of snow like an ice breaker on the lake would do. He went down. He guzzled some beer to help him think as he rehearsed what he would say to the judge. He looked though the wire of a fence and there was Karl. The idiot kid was hitting tennis balls the morning after a snowfall.

Karl bent down to pick up a couple of wet balls when he looked up and saw Mickey plowing his legs through the cliff of snow at the end of the court. Mickey kicked tennis balls out of his path, never taking his eyes off of Karl, who leaned his racket against the bench and waited. "Having a bad time, Mick?" He said it with as much sympathy as he could muster for a bully. He spoke genuinely and in a near-soothing tone tapered to a point by fear as Mahoney drew closer. Karl could see the vapor from Mickey's mouth puffing out a little too rapidly. The staggering was more than called for on the scraped surface of the court. "I mean it," said Karl. "You could use a friend right now, I bet." Mickey was not interested in friendship and said as much. "Why don't you go home and eat your turkey dinner, Daugherty. Go on. Get out of here before I knock you on your ass just 'cause. You just plain irritate me. I don't like you or your holy-assed, stuck up mom or your pretty little sister or your four-flushing cheater of an uncle."

"Sorry but you don't get to tell me where to go or what to do. And, we're having pheasant." Karl was physically bowed up now. After months of repressed yet burgeoning rancor, things would reach a climax. He made ready for the fight, grateful to finally get to it, no matter the outcome. Mickey walked over to the bench, wiped the snow from the edge to set down his quart and snatched up Karl's expensive racket. He took an unskilled backhand and then a sloppy forehand swing, making swooshing sounds with his mouth and wiping snot on his sleeve. "You should take up a real sport, like boxing." He casually swung the racket and hacked it into Karl's eyebrow. There was the sudden explosion of light, abrupt darkness, and a spinning sensation. Blood gushed out of the gash the racket left behind. Mahoney threw the racket to the ground and butted the boy with his shoulder. Karl shoved back and they traded a few punches. Mickey landed a right just to the left of the injured eye, which cleared it of blood for an instant. With his restored eyes, Karl prepared to counter when he lost his footing on the slick court and lay on his back. Mickey kneeled on his chest. Karl laughed at the irony. The drunk had kept his footing perfectly. Mickey reached back high to punch Karl and bowed his head instead as if to begin a Thanksgiving prayer. Karl's eye was full of blood again but he could see Mickey shake his head and slide off of him. "Mickey, I hope you get some help or something. You need help. I never did anything to you. I never even talked bad about you. I've been telling people that they may not know the whole story. Everybody deserves a chance to be heard."

"Yeah, I thought beating on you would make me feel good. To me, one Daugherty was just the same as the other. But I been kidding myself. Your uncle put me in my place. He's tough as nails, and how." Mickey looked out over the golf course for a long time before he got up and brushed caked snow off of his knees. "I'm mad enough to kill somebody today, Karl. I'm going to leave now so it won't be you. You're alright. You got some good fight in you. Me, I'm done."

Later, after the pheasant bones had been picked clean, Sean stayed back with Karl at the Daugherty table, a ruined landscape of leftovers. He poured himself a cup of coffee from Verna's grandmother's silver urn. He had Karl's ear, talking about two different flocks of turkey he had seen. One had been as close as the last bend downhill from the house. The other was in a ruined old settlement eight miles north. "Tomorrow, bright and early I'm going out to Instanter and, I can feel it in my bones, I'll get one of them birds. Too late for your holiday dinner and such as that, of course, but you can always eat turkey. You're off school, so you're welcome to come along." Karl said, "I..." and fell silent. In the background was the faint bustle of the others playing some game in the living room. It sounded like Connor, "Don't look so stunned. I know some answers." You could barely make out Connor's words. There were two quick pops, both barrels of a shotgun firing at the very turkeys Sean had seen about three hundred yards down the hill. The sterile and distant sound made him stir in his chair. Next to enjoying his brother's hearth and feasting with him on this odd holiday in his new country, his favorite place to be was out there crunching on the snow with his shotgun. He imagined himself among the hemlock trees heavy with their snowy burdens and no sound but the wind. But something was all wrong. More time had passed in the unmeasured gap of his hunting daydream. Why had Karl just uttered a single syllable and quit that way? Sean turned to look at his nephew who sat with a vapid stare, his mouth open. Karl's eyes rolled back, showing an unearthly white. He began to quake violently. "Verna, Connor, come here quickly now, Karl has taken a fit!" Sean plied a spoon to Karl's tongue and clasped his jaw to keep him from biting down on it.

4

PRISON UNDER ICE

The week before Christmas was a busy one for the Daughertys. Verna was making wreaths and gift wrapping jars of her own holiday jelly. Eunice had taken on her brother's chores which included chipping ice dams from the roof. She changed her clothes the minute she arrived home from school and went up a ladder with her homemade straight hoe. She got herself into a tango-like rhythm of three steady chops followed by a scraping, then a tossing of loose chips over the gutter. As Sean pulled up to the front porch, a hoe full of ice plopped on the driveway just in front of his truck. Connor was still at work and would be working overtime. Some of his workers at the Elliot Company plant were already on vacation and he had to fill in. He said that there was a big push on to get some clatter out of a new motor design that was in the testing stage. Verna was not expecting him for dinner.

Karl was in his room working on his crystal set. He lifted it from his desk and gave it a light shake. No rattles. When he set it down gently and eased his fingers from beneath it he spoke to it, as he often did. "We need to get you ready for some cold winter nights. Nights when folks have little else to do. I need you." The doctor said that Karl would be out of school for a while, that he needed as much rest as he could get. Verna told him to lie down and try to sleep a little before dinner and he had done as she asked but this was looking like one of his good days, too good to waste in bed. He had plenty of energy and he was walking through open spaces in the house without holding onto things. He said to himself right out loud that he had the world by the ass. But while he tinkered he couldn't deny his mounting choke of frustration. The screwdriver was continually slipping off the heads of the screws. In his mind there was a kind of field servant call-and-answer going on.

You've slipped a screwdriver blade off of screws before. No big deal.

I never had a crippling disease before.

You can still walk, can't you?

Yeah, for how long? You are kidding yourself, boy. Your walking gets wobblier every day. How long before you have to use a goddamn bed pan? Won't that be an encouraging development?

It was call and answer like that for a long while. He still had the screwdriver in his hand. He started tossing it from his left hand to his right, watching it travel the three or four inches from hand to hand. He kept it up for a while to quiet his gloom, ever widening the gap in his hands to five, six, then seven inches apart until the tool skittered across the floor and under the dresser.

Doctor Brenner told him to keep a journal of his symptoms but lately his entries were becoming less and less truthful. Some even strayed completely from descriptions of the sensations of his body. He focused more on the workings of his heart and mind. Verna was reviewing the journal with him every day or two and she encouraged him to write more about wobbliness and hands that don't work just right. When he wrote his entry that morning he was pacing back and forth in his room pausing to look out at the tree line at some busy birds and a waddling porcupine. He wrote a couple of lines, for Verna to read later:

There was only a little numbness on my left side this

morning. No spinning feeling on my way to the bathroom. I tried to picture that mantel piece. I can only imagine how nice it is. Uncle Sean is the best carver in the world. When I think about getting to work on it I feel like it's Christmas Eve and I'm waiting for Eunice to come and help me downstairs.

Karl left the screwdriver under the dresser and returned to the window to think and to study the patch of ground where he had seen that porcupine to see if his tracks were still there. They were gone. He nearly lost his balance completely as his vision blurred and the room rotated around him. He steadied himself with a hand on the window sill until the spell passed.

In the quiet of his room he recalled the earliest signs of his disease. The last time he had been outside for any length of time was a trip he made out tree marking with his cousin Eric. Eric worked part time for a logging operation marking trees with bright yellow paint for pulpwood harvesting. They rode high over the ruts on some fire lines and logging roads into the evening. Eric shot at some deer just before it got dark. He had jumped out of his truck and started blasting. The little herd flashed in and out a thicket of hemlock at a run so it was hard to get a good shot. Karl had one sighted in but the barrel of his gun was stirring the air in slow motion. It was like he was reaming an invisible hole in the space in front of him. He couldn't stop it. He was about to squeeze off a shot anyway but he couldn't quite feel the texture of the gunstock. He took the shells out of his rifle and put the safety on. They drove back out of the deep woods and back toward the hard road. Because of what happened next Karl was overcome with shock. For the entire time the truck ambled among frozen ruts Karl sat wide-eyed. Eric skillfully downshifted and navigated the road, steering around rocks jutting from the snow. The truck's rear-end whined and the wind whipped across the boys' ears. Eric couldn't make out what his cousin had said, though it was apparent that Karl had turned to say something. "What did you say, bud?"

Karl swallowed hard and gripped the stock of his rifle until the color drained from his fingers. He had to look down to see what his left hand was doing. Maybe Eric didn't hear him over the interference of the wind or the roaring exhaust manifold. He sat there with his look of astonishment, staring straight ahead the entire way back to the paved road. He had tried to tell Eric that he couldn't hold the gun steady but only a guttural groan had come out of him like a bad attempt to imitate a lion. He heard it plainly himself and at that moment the groan became a gasp, as though a blast of cold wind took his breath away. Eric said, "I couldn't hear you back there. You ok?" Karl rubbed at his chin a moment, looked straight ahead, and said, "Pff, huh," moaned like he'd been punched hard in his belly, and managed to say, "I'm fine, just tired is all. Let's get home."

Now, back in his ice-covered prison Karl relived the feeling he had in Eric's truck. It came upon him each time he had one of these episodes, like someone kept stuffing him into a concrete box outside of which he could not be heard. There were a few entries in his journal about it. Karl pulled his journal from his desk drawer and paged back to where he had written, "I can't get my words out! My thoughts are clear but when this happens I can't make human sounds."

Karl was reading passages about his frustrations, big and small. Things like a couple of slips with a hand tool don't mean a thing, really. It's a hundred niggling things like missing the light switch or tearing the corner off of a page he tried to turn. He shut his eyes down tight and gritted his teeth. I'm not a cripple yet. He could hear Eunice up on the roof chopping. Karl considered what he would write if he had picked up his pen when he took the journal from his desk: It isn't right that Eunice has to do her own chores and mine too. She doesn't complain a minute but I don't want my sister up on that roof.

He slowly got down on all fours to retrieve the screw driver under his desk when he heard the muffled tones of his uncle talking to his mother downstairs. He couldn't make out what they were saying. The sounds came dampened into murmurs through his floor heat register. He opened his door a crack and stood near it.

He could just make out his mother saying, "What will you have him doing, though?"

"Just some light sanding mostly. He'll be fine, Verna. He loves to work with wood and he's been learning. He has a natural way with it."

"Just don't push him or rush him. He's doing everything a little slower. The things he can still do."

"Don't worry. There's no need. I could finish the mantel without help at all. It's just that, well he takes such pleasure in it himself. I think it will help him, being content, taking his mind off things, you know? Feeling useful. Sick or no, we all need that."

Karl heard his mother sobbing. Whatever this accursed thing was in him, it could kill him and he would go willingly. He was at peace with it. To hear his mother crying over it, that was too much. There was a long pause. Finally she spoke again. "You are so right, Sean. Just be careful. Don't leave his side and no sharp tools. He has trouble." Karl understood that leaving things out of his journal was not fooling Verna a damn bit.

"He'll be fine. We'll finish it all tomorrow and we'll start on something new together, he'll do only what he can manage. That's a promise. Is he up in his room, then?"

Sean came up the stairs. Karl sat swiftly back down and fidgeted with the two-way radio set. Sean knocked twice and opened the door. "Hello sport." Sean looked down at the tubes and wires strung together on Karl's desk and said, "Get yourself a giant megaphone and hold it out the window. No wires. No fancy gadgets that keep failing on you." Karl stood up a little unsteadily to greet his uncle. At that instant they heard a big thud overhead. Sean walked quickly to the bedroom window and threw it open. "You alright up there, darlin?" Karl poked his head out the window next to Sean's. Eunice quickly resumed her tango with the home made chipper and then took a pause as her crimson face poked out over the gutter. "Oh, I'm fine. I only hurt my pride." Karl said, "That's it. Get down from there right now! You got that ladder up out back?"

"I do, but I'm not coming down until I'm through."

"Oh you'll be through alright, if you slide off that roof. I'm getting my coat." Karl made a move to get suited up for roof clearing. Sean clutched his shoulder and he paused. His uncle was looking at him but spoke loud enough for Eunice to hear. "Can I get up there through your dad's window? I'm already wearin' my coat."

Eunice banged her ice chipping tool down on the frozen shingles and scowled in the men's direction. "You two gallant knights can stay where the hell you are. I'm doing this and I'm almost done with it too. Another five minutes…" Karl broke in, "…And you'll be splat on the front yard with a busted neck." Sean took two steps toward Connor's bedroom, gently pushing himself ahead of his nephew. He told Karl, "She's a spirited girl, you've got to give her that but if she falls, it's on us for a couple of bums." Eunice's didn't realize that she had begun to chop harder until chunks of shingle showed up in the ice chips. She could barely hear the men talking below so she guessed at what their chatter might be about. "I heard that! I happen to be perfectly capable of this job. I'm like a cat up here. Don't you dare climb up here. I mean it."

Sean looked at his nephew with an exaggerated double-take. Karl shrugged back at him and they went back and shut the window. She raised her voice again, louder this time to get her words through the pane of glass. "That's more like it. Make me some hot chocolate if you want to do something. I'll be down in a jiffy."

"You heard the lady, Karly, in a jiffy. I'll have a cup too."

In the kitchen Karl cleared some bundles of evergreen sprigs for working space and prepared the hot chocolate. Sean watched him feel along the kitchen cabinets to steady himself on his way back to the table.

Karl settled himself unsteadily onto his seat cushion. Sean gave his nephew a quick silent nod, the kind that says well done.

Satisfied with his nephew's ability to move about unassisted, he got right to his reason for coming. "Karl, my boy," he said, "If I were in your place and couldn't get out much, I believe that the getting out would be its own medicine." He squared up the holiday placemat in front of him to give himself a moment to gather his thoughts. "I still need your help early tomorrow with that mantel if you're up to it. Only if you're up to it. You're the best judge of what you can handle. We'll be getting a very early start. You decide."

"Uncle Sean, a team of draft horses couldn't keep me from it. And I can help. My hands are still pretty good. Don't you worry about me."

"I know it, son. Just making doubly sure. We can always work out another day for it."

Karl studied the three wise men on his placemat with their camels and horses, the exaggeratedly bright star above them. They had the freedom to come and go as they pleased. Why shouldn't he? Then came the frightening idea that if he waits too long he'll never spend another day with his uncle. He started talking so he wouldn't have to listen to those thoughts. "Naw. The sooner the better. Besides, last I saw your mantel it looked finished to me. How hard can the work be? A little varnish? Some stain?"

"Ah, but you only saw her up on saw horses. She's still got all my buried secrets. All my little nasties still lingering, underneath, mostly. But remember, the thing is made to hang above a fireplace where all of that will be open and on constant display."

"Right. You must be doing your finish work from the top down, then. That's why your little nasties are still there."

"Exactly. The broader surfaces are on top, the narrow crannies below are the hardest to get to. It's why, my boy, I'm not a master. A master does the most difficult parts first."

Eunice came in brushing snow from her woolens and pulling off her boots. "Look at the two of you gossiping around the table like a couple of old grannies." She warmed her hands by the burner under the pot of chocolate and milk. She removed the pot and shut off the gas. "This is ready. You two were going to let it get all curdled up, weren't you? That's disgusting. If you want something done right..." Karl got up and poured the steamy cocoa into some mugs with snowmen and reindeer on them. Verna was in the living room with her wreath supplies on a folding card table. She said to Eunice, "Don't you have a theme to write, something about machines and logging operations?"

"Log Skidding and Fatality Rates. I've got all the statistics. No sweat."

"No sweat? Now is that any way for a young lady to talk?"

"It shan't be too laborious," Eunice said, as though she were at high tea, then shifted back to her normal voice. "Seriously Mom, it's two hours of work, tops. I've got all weekend. I'm carrying an A in English anyways."

"Anyways? They need a new English program at that school. But okay, you know best," Verna said, and returned to her craft.

Karl said to Sean, "Mom can make a beautiful Christmas wreath out of a coat hanger and greens but she can't make a lady out of her."

Sean lifted his cocoa in a toast. "I don't know. I find her delightful just as she is." He toasted, "To a delicate flower among the briars."

Karl raised his cup with them and sipped his beverage. "Delicate flower," he repeated. In his head he said, *I hope her grades don't slip because of me.* You could nearly smell and taste the invisible turmoil at that table. Sean finished his mug. "Thank you for the cocoa. See you in the morning."

5

RAW CREVICES

On Saturday morning way before sunrise, Sean picked up a kerosene lantern and asked Karl to follow him into the bedroom of his cabin. Karl looked over his uncle's shoulder, watching as he unlocked an iron lock embedded in a drawer that was built into the base of his bed. He hastily drew out a few packages of sandpaper and a leather pouch folded over on itself with the wooden handles of a fine set of carving knives sticking up out of it. Karl had used them before. They were expensive, handmade carving tools that were smooth and sharp and made him feel like a master when he held one in his hand, so perfectly balanced and sturdy. To Karl they possessed a near-mystical power that could instantly make whoever used them and expert craftsman. He knew this was a silly notion but he indulged the fantasy anyway. Sean said he would keep a set this fine for the rest of his life but if anything happened to him, they would go to Karl. Sean hefted the pouch twice then laid it back in the drawer. He held the sandpaper packets up to the lantern to see if they were the right grit. He seemed in a hurry to start. He handed the sandpaper to Karl, pulled out a pair of heavy shears and laid his keys on the bed. As they walked, Sean snipped the sandpaper packets open.

They went into the back room of the log house where Sean had set up the ornate mantel. It looked so majestic and so weighty resting there on some fat saw horses with drop cloths underneath. That piece was the best carving job Karl had ever seen. It featured some bull elk, bears, deer, and even a mink with three kits in relief. The animals were posed amid trees, bushes and ferns. With detail so remarkable before him, Karl silently accused his uncle of false humility. Not a master? Not much.

The sanding continued steadily for more than an hour. Sean got them some sassafras tea and biscuits and someone came to the door. Karl could hear his uncle talking for a few minutes and he came back, gulped down some tea and said, "Carry on, son. I've got to go look at some beaver pelts in Bud Gorski's barn. Take it easy. Don't push yourself." He leaned over the mantel and rubbed his hand under some scroll work. "You may want to trim under here just a wee bit for me too. "But again," he said, treading backward and out of the room, "We're very close to finishing and we've plenty of time. Pace yourself. We'll lay the first coat of varnish on her before supper."

Karl rubbed the wood into a satin smoothness as his mind wandered. He began to think about his doctor who talked a lot about resting and healthy food. He spoke of fresh air and the benefits of walking out in it with the sun on your face. All of that is fine but what about school and tennis and the wood cutting job he planned to get in the Spring? Doctor Brenner had little to say about those things. Karl didn't trust him because he was a terrible actor. Doc Brenner would hem and haw all day before he answered the boy's really gritty questions, like, "How do other guys do when they get this sickness? How soon do they get better? Is there medicine that works?" Each time it was the same tap dance of whimsy, vagueness and hollow medical talk. Karl quit asking him. And Eunice keeps checking on him and telling him to keep his chin up like that's going to matter, and then she tells him to go ahead and have a good cry and get it out. Nobody would have to know. Which is it Eunie, suffer in silence or have a crying jag?

"No." Karl said it out loud. "Not today." He wouldn't spoil his day with his uncle by being down in the mouth. No more slogging through bitter mud about his trouble. The doctor doesn't know what it is, maybe it's all in his head and he can someday shake it out or work it out. As long as he worked on the mantel he was away from his trouble, whatever the hell it was.

He lay on his back underneath the big mantel. It was so beautiful. It dominated the room, lying in state so imposing, so substantial, even its shadow looked weighty. As he stroked the underside with the rhythm of industry, hard and fast, it never shook or creaked on its saw horse perch. Rock solid and heavy, the mantel was the very picture of a stable fixture. He paused every few minutes for a measured spell in an exploratory waltz of the hands, feeling with his fingertips to see if the nicks and grooves left behind by Sean's tools were erased forever.

Karl worked steadily and steered his thoughts with the rudder of a stoic mind. He would not allow any self-pity to drag him into the same old bitter swamp. With his symptoms completely abated he was in control and his work would take him to a good place where he could enjoy his uncle's approval and stand back with him to admire and be satisfied. There is nothing quite like that kind of satisfaction. The tangible kind, the finished piece, a creation. He got up from the floor and moved the bare light bulb closer to the ornate carvings underneath the left side of the mantel. Huge, towering shadows swept like a skyline across the ceiling. There in the brightness he could see some little shadowy lumps of wood that his uncle's carving had missed. He moved the light over the same position on the mantel's underside on the right. The identical, blocky flaws poked out of the wood where smooth contours should have been.

These hidden imperfections were too much to sand away. He would need to whittle at them. He imagined the worst. He saw himself slipping with a carving knife and putting a big ugly gouge in Sean's work. He worried about having a fit with the tool in his hand and opening up a big gash in himself. He knew about his own seizures only in an alien, second-hand way. He had no personal memory of them. If he had one today at the wrong moment and something bad happened, it would be the last time he would be allowed to work with wood. That time would come soon enough. Doc Brenner tried and failed to gloss it over and Karl's mother was much more artful about it. The truth was that his condition was getting worse. Everyone's silence about it proved that they believed that declining health was his fate, that he would keep getting worse, but nobody would talk to him about it. Even his sister, who was normally so blunt about everything, simply said, "Nobody seems to know what the problem is. How can they know that you won't just get better? If it were me, I would live as much as I can and hope to God my wellness comes back as quickly as my sickness came."

Eunice's advice played like a phonograph record in his head as he walked back into Sean's bedroom. Sean had Bud Gorski wiring the old cabin for him but Bud's work hadn't reached the bedrooms yet. Karl lit a kerosene lamp and took it to his uncle's bed. He slid the bed drawer open and reached in for the pouch of carving knives. His hand brushed something in the back of the drawer which slid back a little farther when his knuckles hit it. He took a reflexive, staccato glance left and right past the glow of the lantern. He rubbed the bottom of his chin and a nervous titter squeaked out. He was looking into darkness and at what? Nobody came in since Sean left. He stopped in mid-reach just for a moment. His breathing became quicker and his mouth dried out. The feeling was the same as the time he stole a handful of chocolate drops from Cliffe's drugstore.

Karl pulled an unadorned wooden box out of the drawer and laid it on the bed. It was the size of a desktop humidor. In the lamp light it was clear what he was looking at. He had seen the box before and the night he first saw it was forever stamped into his mind. There are pivotal experiences that a boy never forgets and a man looks frequently back upon. The events of that night were exactly of that quality.

In the late summer past, he had gone with Sean to Clearfield to the county fair. They watched a thrill show where a man on a motorcycle did loop-de-loops in a giant vertical squirrel cage and jumped through fire and ramped over large wooden barriers. He and his uncle rode on contraptions designed to bubble up boiling batches of fear in your stomach and jazz you up so much, your legs shake under you when they're planted back on the ground. Now that his legs had begun to betray him so frequently, he couldn't help wondering why anyone would evoke that instability on purpose. He rubbed at his chin and put his hands in his pockets, partly because it was chilly in the back of the cabin, and partially because his hands could do no evil while they rested there.

Karl's restraint was admirable but his curiosity was upon him with a sudden fiendishness. He would open that box. He had to.

Toward the end of that August night in Clearfield, Sean took Karl to the hooch show. The boy felt as if he would jump free of his skin but he forced himself to act like it was all as routine as a trip to the Eagan's hardware store. They walked up to a bawdy looking tent with banners showing a harem of dancing girls bursting from their gauzy, billowing blouses. The canvas depicted three dancers in curly blond locks posing behind balloons that barely hid their womanly secrets. Above the dancer's heads were names like Fifi and Scarlet and Desiree in huge gold and crimson letters. The barker in his striped coat and straw hat beckoned the gentlemen who happened by just before show time. "Don't be shy, fellas. You don't want to miss this show tonight. I bring you a little sample, come closer and feast your eyes!" The promoter made a sweeping gesture toward the platform behind him. As he did, flesh and blood sideshow dancers assembled in a row. Music resembling the song of a snake charmer cracked and squealed from tinny loudspeakers on the stage. The three sirens in burlesque dress undulated and shimmied behind the pitch man. Karl was getting stirred up in his body and in his mind. The sparks flew as those exotic ladies danced, igniting his imaginings about what they might perform beyond the stage show.

Sean guided Karl's shoulder to the ticket booth. A plump, sweaty man with a cigar said, "What'll it be for you, pal?"

"Two please," said Sean.

The ticket guy pulled the cigar from his lips and pointed it at a big red and white yard stick on the side of the booth. "If the boy's head is at the mark he can go in." Karl was 16 but kind of a late bloomer. He was waiting for his next big growth spurt, which the inflexible ruler on the ticket booth announced to the world was untimely and may not come at all. Sean fluffed the boy's hair, teasing it into a ball of moss on the crown of his head. He squinted at the marks on the ruler and the illusory improvement in Karl's stature. The ticket seller shook his head with his eyes solemnly shut. Sean drew a folded five dollar bill to the top of his shirt pocket and left its green edge exposed. The carnie went, cigar in hand, back into the ticket shed. Sean slid the price of two tickets under a slot in the glass partition. He slipped his bribe discretely on top of his fee as if covering a bet. "I think this might age the boy slightly, don't you?"

"Move along or you'll hold up the line. Are you going in or not?"

Inside, man and boy waited quietly among the expectant murmur of farm boys, lumbermen, truck drivers, trappers, workers from the dairies and nearby cheese plant. Occasionally you could hear a nervous but lascivious laugh rise above the din. When the first dancer came out with her arrangement of large balloons she wiggled and gyrated to more blaring music distorted in the speakers like what Karl had heard outside. Though the stripper held her props with a triangular handle she slipped once or twice to reveal scanty flesh-colored garments behind them. The audience members toward the back of the tent sipped booze from flasks they passed to each other and cheered and howled all through the show. From the seats in front, the view was disappointing. Amid the strong smell of damp sawdust and whiskey, and under the hot lights, the balloon dancer looked older than she had out front and her carelessness had not produced the breech in modesty that was advertised. Karl made a comment on this duplicity in whispers with Sean. Sean said, "It's a carnival Karl, everything's bright and puffed way up like the spun sugar. But you must admit, the old gal has some good steps. She's just the first. They'll get prettier as we go along." Then he stood and said, "And there will be a fine finale. Wait till you see it! I've got something I need to do. Meet me outside the gate by the ticket booth after the show."

After Sean went out through the exit, Karl watched the woman for a few minutes more. The milkmen in the back grew louder and more unruly. Karl saw two big guys with tattooed arms and night sticks join a third man near the exit. The boy lingered to see if the dancer would reveal anything as promised by the booster out front. Gradually the thrill gave way to disgust and dread. His fool's dream evaporated. The spike of an erection had withered down and been replaced with a dull ache and a whiff of nausea. Gone were his imaginings of that other kind of dance she might have after the last show. Now another kind of trouble would erupt in the tent with the roustabouts swinging their clubs and busting heads. Karl sat up stiffly then jumped to his feet. He decided to pass politely in front of the guys sitting in his row and leave his last hooch show behind him.

Karl didn't know what business his uncle Sean had nor where he had gone to conduct it. He stood among the cheap calliope music coming out of the carousel and the sick sweetness of the cotton candy booth. Scanning 360 degrees of fairgrounds, he didn't see Sean so he counted off fifteen steps directly ahead of him and from there he smelled roasted peanut and hot sausage smells. The burlesque strains coming from the balloon dancers' tent had faded completely. He repeated his progress a third time and now he could see a wire fence and beyond it, several travel trailers and smaller camping tents. There was a large bus with a green and white striped awning and lights on inside just past some picnic tables. He noticed a man exiting the bus who looked like Sean but in the darkness he couldn't be sure. The man carried a wooden box under his arm. It was the box that lay on the bed before him now, the same box that he had placed on his own lap on the ride home from the Clearfield fair that Summer night.

Karl recalled the strangeness of the evening at the fairgrounds. He had a clear image of the bubble dancer and the lecherous rabble in the hooch show tent. He remembered something odd about his uncle's reaction when he asked him what was in the box while they were driving home.

"Some delicate carvings and some decorative porcelain eggs," his uncle had told him. A guy from the old country has asked me to find buyers for them, that's all." And when Karl began to open the lid of the box, his uncle spat out a loud command, "Don't open it!" Sean's fervency seemed to startle him as much as it had Karl who slammed the lid back down before he could open it enough to see inside. His uncle calmed his voice and said, "That stuff is just very fragile and, well, I'm responsible. It's expensive and those things have been in that guy's family for more than a century. You understand, don't you?"

"Sure. I was just curious. I didn't mean nothing."

"Course you didn't. Maybe when I get someone interested, you can be there and see them on display. It's nice work, figurines, and such. You'll appreciate them for certain."

But Karl never heard about the stuff in that box again. He had never completely put it out of his mind but he didn't spend much thought on it either. It was just part of a muddle in his memory about that trip to the fair. That is, until this moment with the box resting on the rugged green woolen blanket before him.

Karl set the carving tools next to the base of the hurricane lantern. The lid of Sean's box threw a shadow on its contents. Karl moved the lantern to the left, knocking the pouch of knives to the wooden floor. He quickly picked them up and held them to the light. No damage. Good. He sat on the edge of the bed and looked inside. There were two folded pieces of paper. One was a dry cleaning order sheet under the logo of SPM Industrial Linens – South Portland, Maine. The paper was course and faded. There was an intricate drawing of a cargo ship, afloat across a letter V. The order form was a blank checklist of goods and services. Karl turned the slip over and there were three columns of nonsense words next to each other in a table. He slid the flap of a small brown envelope open to find a locker key with F-2 engraved on one side and 23 on the other. The brand name on it was Ideal. He removed an off-white bundle of linen napkin material ringed in bailing wire. He untwisted the wire and removed the cloth to reveal four cylinders half again as big around as an unfiltered cigarette and approximately the same length. Each one had a pair of wires, white and blue, protruding from one end like a very long double fuse on a firecracker. The cylinders were stamped on the side with *Sprengkapsel*.

He studied the three columns again and decided to copy them on the back of a sheet of sandpaper. With the copy of the coded material safely in his pocket he began to return the strange items to the wooden box.

Karl froze up and lost his grip on the odd bundle of cylinders. It tumbled to the bed. He had heard a loud thump outside and the whistling of a strong gust of wind. Another gust blew in and with it a second noise as the hint of a dark bristly hemlock bough brushed the top of Sean's bedroom window frame. He rewrapped the metal firecrackers in their gauzy package, careful to twist the bailing wire around them precisely as he had found it. He compared the back of his sandpaper to the list of gibberish one last time then put the original copy and the metal cylinders back in the box like he had found them. He slipped the locker key into his pocket, returning its empty envelope. "No one will be the wiser," he whispered. Karl's snooping and its taint of dishonor could remain tucked into the darkness of the bed drawer as long as nobody knew of it.

The boy quenched the wick of the lantern and bristling goose bumps gave him pause. Immediately upon reading them like Braille on his arms he became wobbly and heard a buzzing sound in his ears. "Goddamn it!" he said through his teeth. Karl's body was sending him a threatening message like it had done so many times before. He expected next to fall to the floor and wake up sometime later with a headache and sore muscles. He would feel tired but not know at first where he was or what he had been doing or how much time he had lost. He stood in the dark alone for what seemed to be half an hour. Then he mumbled a short prayer of thanks because this time the threat was no more than a tease. His supplication was interrupted rudely when the silence was pierced by footfalls on the front steps. Uncle Sean! He gasped and rushed, running over an eggshell path to the back room where he slid himself under the mantel and took a carver's tool to the roughness underneath it.

Sean stood in front of his work with Karl's legs poking out from beneath it. After a pause in which the only sound was the chunking away of small furrows of wood. Sean said, "I'm guessing you found my little nasties there, Karl."

"Well I… what do you mean?" His mind raced and vaulted to a set of disquieting conclusions. Sean must have seen the lamplight coming from his bedroom window. The sun was just beginning to come up. Karl was convinced that it would throw dramatic backlighting on some direful revelation. He was certain to be face-to-face now with his uncle in a showdown about the real contents of that box he had locked up in his bedroom. The boy hoped against hope that there was some innocuous explanation, that he wasn't really carrying this burden of knowledge – *Oh, God please let me be wrong!* - because if he was right, his Uncle Sean was up to his neck in something underhanded and evil. There was a lot of talk about the fifth column on the radio, in the magazines, in the newsreels, the cinematic cliché of spies in their dark suits and shifty eyes in the camera lens. The whole country was on watch and urged to report any suspicious activity. In his mind, anything the Nazis would try to pull would be more suited for New York or Philadelphia. What could they possibly have to do with Ridgway? But then he began to see the posters, like the ones in the Post Office and at the Elk County courthouse. One showed a seagoing freighter upended in the ocean. Underneath was a caption, *Loose Lips MIGHT Sink Ships*. And another, with its spooky, beady-eyed German infantryman caricature peering out from under a distinctly German helmet, *He's Watching You*. What would Karl say to his uncle now, since he didn't know exactly what the questionable content of that box really meant? Those props, straight out of a cheap cloak-and-dagger mystery comic book. Then as Karl was groping for the answers Sean spoke again, "I mean of course, my little nasties, the rough cuts under the scrollwork. We'll be on those for hours."

Karl's sigh was so deep and his exhale so forceful that fine wood dust billowed out from the carvings of mink as though they were breathing out puffs of vapor into the frigid air. His shoulders released their tension and rested squarely on the floor. Weakly he replied, "I bet so, Uncle Sean." There was little of the teenage enthusiasm Sean expected to hear in his nephew's voice.

"Well, do you need another short rest? You sound kind of winded."

"Oh, no. I'm ok. I got a cramp, that's all."

Karl's relief had him frozen in that moment. He stalled about as long as recovery from cramping should take. A confrontation had been averted. As sure as the woods around Sean's cabin would fill with sunlight in a few minutes, a time would come when they would face off. It would be nothing like the way he imagined.

6

THE BATTLE OF THE WISE - PART 1

I
t was a Wednesday in early February, 1943 and Karl was sitting
on the hearth, its embers glowing orange-red and the oak logs
shifting and cleaving with a thud. He had built that fire just
after dawn and had it blazing pretty well before his mother left for
her errands. Now he would have to interrupt his studies to go out
to the porch for more wood. Karl was alone in the house reading a
series of articles about ham radio receivers. This was an off day.
He was slow. It took close to an hour to fold each Popular
Mechanics and Radio News at the opening page of each article and
stack them in order on the stone hearth beside him. His hands
were in a conspiracy against his brain. They colluded to drop the
magazines and make folds in the wrong places. He stopped and
cried for a few minutes. It was ok to cry. Verna was in town
getting groceries and new sheets and pillow cases. She was also
buying Karl a toilet seat with a bucket under it for his bedroom.
See if I ever use that... that cripple's toilet, he thought as he
fumbled with the magazines, reading material that his mind was
snapping up in large spade-loads. Soon Eunice would have to hold
them for him and turn the pages. He felt the numbness on the left
side of his body. It was too much. But then he took a
handkerchief in both hands and cleaned his nose and dried his
eyes. He heard a metallic clanking, the closing of a truck door just

outside. Then the sound of boots scuffling across the welcome mat. Sean came in with a wad of currency in his hand. He put it on the kitchen table with a slam that upset the pepper shaker, a pilgrim man figurine which had been keeping vigil in the center of the table since November. Sean set the Quaker statuette back on its feet and said, "It's payday. Sixty-five dollars. Beil took delivery this morning and he was very happy at that. He's building some new offices on his property and wants me to trim out the whole place. You got a five dollar bonus for the finishing work, a piece of my own bonus for that superb and lovely mantel."

Karl looked at his uncle, who was smiling broadly and congratulating himself in the glare of the kitchen window. Karl tried to get up but changed his mind. He didn't want Sean to see the elaborate series of maneuvers rising from the hearth would require. He decided to talk from where he sat. When he opened his mouth he heard an ungodly growling sound. What he intended to say was, "Thanks for dropping off my pay." The frightful wolf-like snarl was like a gunshot. It shattered the joy of their payday. Sean sprang forward out of the backlit glare and caught him just before his shoulder crashed into the fireplace grate. Karl heard the clanging sound of the coal shovel and iron poker he had knocked over on the stonework. In a minute his seizure had passed and Sean lifted him and sat him in an overstuffed chair. Karl couldn't tell if an hour or a minute had passed and he didn't know if his eyes were open, just that everything was black. Then a small tunnel of light opened like a pinhole. The scope of his vision widened slowly until he saw things normally. He was sitting in dull quiet, looking at Sean who asked him, "How are you feeling, Karl?" Karl decided to answer with his gratitude. The dullness persisted as he formed his thoughts into words, which had become much more labored, like pushing his father's push mower with its brake still on. "What I meant to say Unc was, I appreciate it. Wow! Sixty five bucks! I'll have the best radio in town."

"I tink we should get you to the doctor. I'll leave a note for your mother."

"I tink you're right." Sean ignored Karl's mocking tone. He

42

could see the boy's difficulty in uttering a few simple words. At the same time he noticed his nephew struggling to rise and giving up. This was nothing new. What was different was the look of terror in Karl's eyes, so much so that his uncle turned to look behind him to see what he was so afraid of.

There was no ghost or lunatic with an ax approaching. The contortions in Karl's face were from his being tugged at inside. He loved Sean like a brother and he hated the useless invalid he was himself becoming. The bad days were more frequent now, Karl could not deny it, but worse, he was horrified by the real little nasties and the treason they seemed to represent, these things that couldn't be filed down, or cut, or sanded away. Something had to be done about it and soon.

Sean drove him into town. The doctor visit was the same as so many before it. The only difference was that Sean sat on a bench just outside of Brenner's examination room where he could keep one eye on the receptionist, who was one of the most beautiful young women in town. Her name was Cleo Armstrong. They had not been formally introduced but once he was sure that his nephew was taken care of, he intended to introduce himself and see where that went. He would pretend to read the waiting room copy of For Whom the Bell Tolls. Hemmingway was a safe choice to show Cleo his refined taste. He kept an ear trained on the dialog beyond the flimsy curtain across Brenner's examination room doorway. Doctor Brenner made notes and checked Karl's eye movements. He asked the boy some silly questions. The answers were no problem, it was saying them. Stuttering, stammering and finally giving up, he had answered them immediately in his head. "What's five plus two?"

"Ssss. Sss. Sev."

And then, "Who won the World Series?"

"Drrrr. Aeeyynnn… duh-eerg." Sean overheard him through the curtain. He was nearly certain that the boy had managed to sputter out "ein dearg," red birds in Irish. But that was absurd because Karl knew no Irish and, as far as his uncle knew, in the midst of his own new fascination with the sport, the Saint Louis Cardinals were not involved in that contest; both of last year's series contenders were teams from New York City. Karl struggled. He began to puff out his lips, looking over at the doctor, then finally, pounded his knees in frustration. Spittle sprayed out of his mouth and onto the black leather of the examination table. Doctor Brenner waited for him with his head tilted back, eyes blinking. He removed his glasses and dropped them into his white coat pocket. "Take your time, son. The Series?"

Karl's tongue was stuck in neutral, trying to say, "It was the goddamn New York Yankees! Who do you think it was?" That was the exact phrase he had mentally prompted himself to deliver. Nothing came out of him except saliva and a few syllables, an unbroken code with no discernable relation to his thoughts. Recalibrating, he tried to say, "I can't do it," but that was futile too. Finally, he walked, or half-fell across the room to a water fountain and took a long drink. He stood in front of the fountain, water running off his chin and soaking his shirt. He stared at Brenner with a quizzical look, head cocked to one side. There in front of Brenner he drooled like an idiot. His eyes pleaded. The old doctor had seen that look many times. Karl was not the only one who had used it to say: "Doctor Brenner, why can't you help me?"

The doctor put his glasses back on and escorted Karl back to the exam table. "Now Karl, I would like to ask a couple more questions before you go. If you still have trouble answering them in the conventional way, with your mouth, can you raise your right hand for yes and your left for no?"

Karl quickly jabbed his left hand in a Hitler salute for an emphatic No! Then he waved both hands in front of himself like a magician introducing an illusion. This was to complete his small joke that amused only him. Humor born of pain often has a short trajectory, an arrow shot directly into the dirt. He waited a moment then he calmly raised his right hand and nodded at the doctor. He attempted to exude a tranquil confidence like George Raft playing Scarface and to show the deftness of his limbs, and could the kind doctor please go on with his questions?

Doctor Brenner went through his series of questions about Karl's chief symptoms, how long he had been having them? More than one day? Yes. More than one week? and so on, and how long they lasted, and other questions about his ability to use the bathroom, and feed and dress himself.

Then the doctor asked him if he was having odd experiences that scared him or upset him in any way. Karl gave Brenner a no signal which was a lie. That very morning as he was lying awake he saw a man in his bedroom wearing a Weedville Dairy shirt, speaking German to him. Karl had somehow crossed a line with this milkman, a line dividing the stuff of nightmares and cold hard reality. It was definitely in the class of things Brenner had just asked him about. He was terrified of what this odd messenger had come to tell him, a wild tale of three men from Maine asking where they could find Karl and his uncle. These men wanted them both dead. It made no sense, since Karl didn't know a word of German, yet he had talked to the German milk truck driver for more than fifteen minutes. Karl lied via hand signals about the apparition which was entirely too complex to convey. Then he distinctly heard the doctor call him a lame brain even though Doctor Brenner's lips were not moving. He held his arms tight to his sides so he wouldn't take a swing at the doctor. He took a few deep breaths. This was not the first time Karl believed that he could hear other people's thoughts. Another flow of angry nonsense. It was meant to say, "I was a wreck when I came in here and I'm going to leave here the same way. Who's the lame brain?"

He sat on the leather, waffling between terror and clear reasoning. Karl gritted his teeth until his jaw ached. This was what his life had become, confusion about what was real, anger over what was happening to his body and fear to the point of shuddering, *if this keeps up I'm going to be trapped in a broken body and never get out.* The brief moment of soundness he had in Brenner's office ended as quickly as it had come with this terrifying thought. then, , his poisoned mind took him to a different place. He began to think that Sean and the doctor were conspiring against him. The fearful shivers passed. In their place was a cool headed resolve to keep certain things quiet until he could sort them out. He realized at that moment that if he had more visions like he had that morning, and he let anyone know, nobody would believe a word of his story about Sean.

The last question Doc Brenner asked was, "Do you need a wheelchair to get to your uncle's truck?" His left hand shot up and waved at the doctor. It was the whimsical, flittering finger sort of wave. The kind you would do for a departing infant. "Bye, bye now you inept little guy in a white coat." It gave him precious little satisfaction to so eloquently insult his doctor, to pronounce each word inside himself with precision and verve. Karl rehearsed these lines in muted echoes inside himself over and over. This was a new habit he had begun to cultivate. Saying snide things to people but never aloud. For a polite country boy, who learned his manners from a proper Swedish woman, saying these things should have been unthinkable, but ironically Karl believed that he was getting to a place where everything was becoming unspeakable; therefore, everything became thinkable by default. *I can say anything I please in my mind and no one is the wiser.* His silent echoes, even nasty ones, were treasures. They offered solace.

Karl walked in a tight circle for the doctor deliberately and carefully. He had barely slept for a week and in the bright light of the examination room he had the sensation that everything was slowing, grinding down to a low idle -- different parts of his personal power, all at different rates. But his lap around the floor tiles betrayed no real sign of incapacity. When he finished he mimed open hands at his sides at the climax of an impressive magic trick, *viola! I can damn well walk.*

*   *   *

When Karl got back home he played some charades with Sean to indicate that he wanted him to bring a pad and paper into his room. Sean found them for him and laid them on the night table. Karl tapped his chest and made a thumbs-up gesture to his uncle. Sean held a finger up and spoke slowly and excruciatingly clearly as if Karl was either deaf or had little cognitive capacity. In mid-sentence Sean realized how mistaken all of that was. He turned and left. Karl slapped himself twice on the sides of his head above the temples, deriding his uncle in pantomime behind his back.

With Sean bumping around and bopping his boot heels down in the kitchen, Karl took measure of his life. There were some things that were still positive. He was not dead, and he couldn't be sure he would be soon, as his sister had pointed out. Karl was strangely comforted. Contentment was his latest mood among several that day. He left the bitterness and anger behind because he didn't know who he should be angry at. Who could he blame? Mickey Mahoney? God? Doctor Brenner? Blaming was not going to make him well. He also realized that he could still make good gestures to communicate and he could still write fluidly. His hands got numb a little now and then but he could write for hours if he needed to. The thought of writing and what he may be required to write about triggered the image of a patriotic poster he had seen somewhere. He concentrated for a minute and recalled in detail the American GI's picture in the foreground and the illustrator's lettering job around him which read:

"The Battle-Wise Infantryman
is careful of what he says or writes.
How About You?" [1]

Karl shook his head, trying to free himself from a muddle. He was unsure of why he recalled that slogan just then but decided that he was too tired to worry about it. He returned to his blessings inventory, a useful device his mother taught him to employ on sleepless nights. Most of all, Karl thought, I don't need that pissed up, half-rotted wheelchair. Not yet anyway. He closed his eyes and fell immediately into a deep sleep.

Karl's dream was as vivid as his fatigue was strong. He was sitting in the Strand movie theatre which was fairly normal looking except that it had a leaky roof. The constant sound of dripping water came from the back of the auditorium as a newsreel played. The auditorium was pitch dark but Karl still had the sharp vision a soldier might have while using and anti-aircraft searchlight.

There was an obvious vertical seam in the center of the screen.

[1] Poster by Jes Wilhelm Schlaikjer, U.S. War Dept., 1944

A man who looked and dressed like Sean Daugherty was reading a newspaper a few seats down the row. There was a tall, bearded, muscle-bound man on screen in a spotless white gymnast uniform who leaned forward into the camera lens until his face distorted. He looked to Karl like a circus strong man. The bearded strongman motioned over his shoulder with his thumb toward a portrait of a German dressed for combat with a newspaper covering his nose and mouth. The gymnast said, "He's watching you." Karl jumped up from his seat which sprung back with a loud banging sound. He looked around the theatre, fearing that the noise would disturb the others. The dozen or more movie patrons didn't stir. They were all dead. Karl was running as fast as he could toward the Exit light. The dripping of water went faster as he ran harder. Water was getting deeper and splashing with each footfall but his feet were dry. He kept running but he drew no closer to the door. It was as if he were on a watery treadmill. On either side of him were beautiful, tall, slender young women dressed provocatively like cigarette girls in a nightclub. Their skirts were short and their blouses low-cut. Like cigarette girls, they had trays slung across their necks with leather straps lined with cotton. On their trays they carried rows and rows of cigarettes that looked to be made of mirror-finish steel. The girls ignored his struggle to escape and the prettier of the two went to the man from Karl's row who was reading the paper. She sold him three of her cigarettes tied in a bundle. He stood, put the metal cigarettes in his pocket and glanced over at Karl, who was bent over, sweating and gasping for breath, exhausted to the point of collapse. Then the man went back to reading his newspaper.

When Karl woke up hours later, Eunice was standing at the foot of his bed.

"I heard you yelling. Are you alright?"

"I'm okay. Is Uncle Sean still here?"

"Nope. He was gone when I came in."

"Mom?"

"She's at the church. Something about a ridiculous Lutheran youth club Valentine's party. She's making me go to it. What a waste of a Saturday night."

"Listen. Shut the door."

Eunice shut her brother's bedroom door and hurried to the side of his bed. "What is it, Karl? You seem a little scared."

"I'm not scared. But who knows? Maybe I should be. I think our uncle is in some kind of serious trouble."

7

THE BATTLE OF THE WISE - PART 2

Eunice went quiet. She wondered what sort of trouble would be too serious for her Uncle Sean. He was tough, nearly crude, yet smart and self-confident, independent, a potent force of a man whom she looked up to as much as Karl did. She was sure there was nothing her uncle couldn't do.

Karl told his sister about the trip to the Clearfield fair in the Summer and the way Sean had had become so agitated when the boy tried to take a look at that innocent box of carvings and porcelain knickknacks that Sean brought home. He explained how he had quite accidentally found out why their uncle had been so protective, so secretive about the box.

"Karl. Why would you go snooping around in Uncle Sean's bedroom like that? That's kind of a rotten thing to do, isn't it?" Her voice betrayed a quiver. There was a plea pushing Eunice's words out. Karl's illness was the source of her anger and her doubt but at times like this she appeared to be angry at her brother. She couldn't be sure that Karl was looking at things right. Since he had begun to have seizures he had, after all, seen some things that were not there; he said he could hear what people were thinking and he had crazy, vivid dreams. Maybe he was confused. Did he dream these things too?

"Rotten or no, I was suspicious, see? On the way home from the fair I just wanted to look at the pretty trinkets his friend from the old country asked him to unload. I figured they were hot and, wrong as that was, I was curious as to why Uncle Sean would agree to do that. He said the carnival guy was a friend of a friend who lives in Ireland, oh, what was his name? And Unc owed the friend in Ireland some payback on a big favor."

"What kind of favor?"

"I remember the guy's name now. He was from someplace near Ulster. Felan Donleavey. His real name is Felan but everybody called him Tom."

"So what? What was the favor?"

"Donleavey paid for Uncle Sean's passage. I'm pretty sure that Tom Donleavey was involved in The Troubles. I can feel it in my bones, Eunie. And if he's that good a friend to Sean Daugherty then Sean Daugherty was involved in The Troubles too."

"You don't know that. Uncle Sean never said…"

"I'm sure he has his reasons for keeping all that under his hat."

"Well they can't be bad reasons, like Uncle Sean is some kind of thug hiding his dark past and sneaking around." Eunice's voice got louder and slightly higher in pitch. "I don't care what they do over there," she said. "That's their problem."

"You know as well as I do, it's a different world these days, Eunie. Anyway, relax. This whole thing could be nothing. I'm not saying anything bad about our uncle here. We've got a ways to go to get to the bottom it. Let's just wait and see."

Eunice thumbed the pages of the note pad on Karl's night stand. She thought about how much fun arguing with her brother used to be. Not anymore. Sometimes he showed her she was dead wrong about a thing but she kept on just to keep him going. She looked at her brother in his bed. It was the middle of the afternoon and he should have been at the country club or at the YMCA hitting tennis balls or something. Was he finished with the things he loved forever? He was rested up now and he was having no trouble talking. Maybe he was getting better. Maybe he would be himself again soon. Eunice was content to just keep talking. She said, "You know what I wonder about sometimes? Dad and Uncle Sean are so different. And have you noticed, they don't have any friends in common? Yeah, they go out hunting and fishing together but they seem so apart from each other."

"Dad doesn't have any Catholic friends. Some people accuse him of being a Unionist or worse, an Englishman even. Sean has all kinds of friends. There are many Irish in town who hate our father. The ones from the plant would have beat the shit out of him a dozen times if he didn't out-rank them. He's their supervisor. They'd be fired."

"They better not beat him up! I'd get my shotgun after them and that would be it. Goodbye fish-eaters! Bastards."

"Young lady! Watch your language. They ain't tweety birds you know. You'd go to prison or get the chair for that. Don't be silly." Eunice shoved at Karl's shoulder as she laughed at him, a coarse grain running through her laughter. She said, "You grew into stodgy old fart overnight. Young lady?"

"Uh, now, back to my point. What was my point?"

"You were talking about guys beating Dad up at work."

"Dad can handle himself. Don't you worry. And if it comes to it, I can't shoot a rifle anymore but we could get a few sticks of dynamite."

"Dynamite? Where would we get any dynamite? Besides, last July Fourth you burned your fingers with a cherry bomb. Lucky you didn't blow them off your hand. What damage could you do with dynamite?" Eunice was enjoying the banter again. This talk of dynamite was all childish hyperbole which took her back in time to Karl telling stories under a bed sheet tent with a flashlight.

Karl said, "Are you serious? You just did that report about lumberjacks. They blow up stumps and stuff all the time. You got a short memory. Anyway. Eunice, quit playing the half-wit sister. Did you ever wonder why our uncle can go out drinking any damn where he pleases?"

"Um, he doesn't have a wife?"

Karl kept on, not acknowledging her answer. "He gets into fights sometimes but afterward he's got his arm over the shoulder of the other guy whose butt he just kicked and orders up a whiskey for him."

"I've never seen it for myself but, yeah, I've heard the stories. You know I have." Eunice was pretending to be hurt by her brother's unfair and unfounded Pollyanna image of her. It was all terribly ironic, his telling her first not to be silly, and then not to be half-witted, remarks she would normally take in stride. But it saddened her to have to doubt Karl. She had a hunch that he wasn't just being crazy this time. For the moment she was content to follow her hunch and forget about the confusion that was giving her a headache. She decided to return to her playful verbal combat. Humor was often her soothing place. "How come you keep asking me stuff you already know the answers to?"

"I'm just trying to get you to use your pretty little head for something besides a hat rack. Now listen. Did you ever wonder how come Dad and Uncle Sean are always arguing? There's something big and ugly between them. Shoot, they both come from Armaugh. They went to the same school, worked in the orchards together."

"I didn't think about it. They're brothers. You and I argue all the time because you think you know everything."

"I know that you don't pay attention to things. Dad says Uncle

Sean is contrary, *contrary and rebellious* is his phrase. You have ears too."

"See, you're doing it again! You're giving me a headache."

"Eunice Daugherty. The so-called pain in your head is from laziness. You're every bit as smart as me but just in different things. If your head truly hurts you, you can take some of Mom's powders later. They're in the medicine cabinet. Think, girl. Sean Daugherty is contrary to what and rebellious to whom?"

Eunice squeezed the sides of her head and groaned. "Aaahhh! You can't help yourself. Why don't you just come out and say it? Tell me what and who."

"Fair enough then." Karl tucked his chin thoughtfully into his palm and braced to deliver profundity to his sister. She didn't wait for the wisdom she knew he was about to impart. "You know, Mom always says we should forget about The Troubles and forgive people and all that. But I think we need to think about The Troubles so we don't behave the same way all over again."

"See that!" Karl said, "I told you. You're the smartest. Why are you wasting your time in that school? Go on to college now."

She wiped her eyes with the shoulder of her blouse. "I didn't come by it from gypsies."

Karl reached out and hugged his sister. She couldn't remember the last time he had done that. It wasn't that she didn't like it but hugging just hadn't been in their mutual lexicon for years. He smiled so broadly she thought he might burst. That smile sent her over a kind of cliff. Tears welled up in her eyes against her resolve never to cry in front of him. He had a sadness of his own. He didn't need her blubbering all over him. "What an extraordinary day. Who can help themselves on a day like this?"

"It is a great day and I won't waste it on my game of twenty questions. I'll give it to you straight. That stuff I saw in that box was code. I'm giving the copy I made to you. You will find it with my radio tools, folded up small and tucked into the box that holds my soldering iron. There's a locker key in there too. You'll need that." Karl sat up and put his pillow behind his back. "You are going to be like a G-man now. You are going to find out some things. Or is it, uh, G-Lady?"

"I guess G-Lady will have to do," Eunice answered.

Karl picked up a pen and began writing his instructions down in a numbered list. He said them as he wrote.

"One. Go to every place in town that has lockers, safety deposit boxes, cigar humidors, or locking cabinets and try to match an Ideal brand lock with a key inscribed with an F-2 and a 23.

Two. Go see Kevin Barry. Tell him I'm running a Lutheran Youth scavenger hunt from my room here and he needs to try to break that code.

Three. Go to the library and look up Sprengkapsel in a German/English dictionary."

"Karl. This is scary. What if we find out that our uncle is involved in something really bad, something dirty and… criminal?" What if he goes to prison or gets deported?"

"All very good questions. Believe me I've been scratching my head about this too. All I know is that Sean Daugherty is a good man. He's always been good to us both and he works hard and he don't take nothing from nobody. I always thought I wanted to be like him when I grow up. If I do grow up. If I get the chance I'm going to ask him what all this is about but I want to know the answers first. I just want to hear his answers before he figures out that I know them. Seems to be the best way to operate."

Eunice was pulling apart inside, swelling with pride and shrinking in fear. Beneath those two feelings there were a dozen other emotions and a single thought which came like a winter wind and froze up everything in her soul. She heard all of Karl's words, the ones about Sean and what was loveable and admirable about him, the ones about Karl's methods and style of acting on things.

She couldn't take exception with Karl's swagger, his intelligence. There was much to be said about a boy who knows who he is and what he stands for. This is what made her so proud, knowing that he would stand by her and her family no matter what. The feelings about Sean and this new revelation were clustered together in their own fiery mass, roaring into a destructive force and demanding to be extinguished. She would ignore that conflagration for now because a thick wave of fear overtook her at that moment. Karl had said, *If I do grow up.* Close behind this first chilling phrase was another, *If I get the chance…* Karl was speaking openly what her insides had forbidden him to say, what her heart refused to accept. Her ears had already let those words flood in despite her bulwarks against them. She couldn't drain them away.

"You can't think that way, Karl. You can't say that." She began to sob and suddenly gave a loud, "Awww good God!" She slapped the backs of her hands on her thighs, palms open, she calmed herself. Her spine straightened and lips pursed with resolve. "Look at me." She sniffed and mopped away tears. "I'm such a baby. But you can't say that, Karl. You are not going anywhere. You're going to get better, I just know it. You'll see."

"I might. But let's say I don't. What then? See, I'm glad you're here right now. If I didn't tell somebody this stuff I would have exploded. It turns out that you are the somebody I needed to tell and that's perfect. You're blood and, you little shit, I can actually trust you." Karl stood up a little swifter than he had all day. There was no wavering or tottering. He merely felt a numbness in his left arm and leg and he had an odd dullness in his sight that lasted a minute after he arose from the bed. He spoke soberly and clearly with very little of the distortion and impediment he had faced at Brenner's office. "There's more. Can you take it?"

"Course I can. What do you think? I'm made of the same stuff you are, Karl Daugherty. I just can't shut down the waterworks some days. Chalk it up to the foibles of womanhood."

Karl sat back on the edge of his bed. He closed his eyes and shut out a few seconds of the light from his window. Then he pushed on his cheeks with both hands as though directing the angle of his jaw might assure control over his power of speech. He did this often and unconsciously and Eunice knew that he was preparing himself for another important statement. He was bridling himself. He finally said, "I have never talked about this to a soul before. Partly because I didn't want to believe it myself and partly, well, I was a kid and I didn't think I had the smarts to figure it out, the confidence in what I saw — not enough to say a word because it's serious."

"Serious in what way?"

"Serious in a way that you don't go around making accusations without some kind of real reason to. Do you know what I mean?"

"Sure I do."

"Even if you think a guy is rotten and sick in the head. Even if you hate somebody. It's not honorable. And worse, if everybody knows the guy is no friend of yours, then you say something and then it's... well, they never did get along so, take it with a grain of sand."

"Salt."

"What? Salt? You want some pepper too?" Karl was a little insulted by her correction. You want to catch a bird? You can shoot it. It's much easier."

"No, you goofy buzzard, take it with a grain of salt." Eunice called her brother a buzzard because she was not allowed to say bastard. "Now, please excuse my English lesson. Go on." Eunice had completely gotten past her weak sobbing and was back to her customary spunk. This made her brother smile. He allowed himself a small giggle and he sobered again quickly.

"Thank you. I never talked about it because I thought I could be wrong. But, it hit me on Thanksgiving day when I had that run-in with Mickey Mahoney. Remember the day of Grandpa's burial. You and I went to our fishing spot? I told you there was something wrong about that whole deal. Mickey had on his hunting hat. Red and black checkers and a yellow fishing license pinned to it. On the side. A 1941 fishing license."

"So? A hat with a fishing license?"

"Mickey Mahoney's hat. Back to my story about Thanksgiving. I was dizzy from getting knocked around. But I saw it clear as the nose on your face. It all came back like a dream. Eunie, he was there the day Grandpa drowned. Mickey went past in a truck and I saw him. I'm pretty sure he saw me too. I must have got back to Grandpa's spot on the river only a few minutes after he went in. He wasn't cold yet. I wasn't gone looking for grasshoppers all that long anyways. I heard that company truck. Big fifty gallon drums banging around in it, and it was definitely Mickey driving it. And I saw him going around the bend in a hurry and in that same checkered hat. I couldn't make out who but there was another guy in the truck with him too. I don't know why he would do it but he did it. He killed Grandpa."

"But Karl. He could have been fishing or doing something else along the river. Maybe he was picking greens or leeks or checking traps or something."

"There were no trap lines out there. That's not where he had been trapping. The way Grandpa's reel was smashed, the way he looked, all beat up. The water wasn't that swift right there, it doesn't make sense. There were more footprints on the side of the river than when I left to get our bait, deep tracks squashed down in the mud. Somebody beat on grandpa and threw him into the river. The cops didn't even go out there. Warren Armstrong gave his statement when the rescue squad pulled the body out and that was it."

"Why didn't anybody look into it?"

"I don't know. Laziness? Stupidity? Hell, Warren went straight to the hose hall for a few stiff drinks right after. I heard he made his official report in a booth at the damn hose hall. That guy barely got through high school. He's kind of slow. You know that. And everybody just figured Grandpa was old and he wasn't so spry. That's nuts. I could hardly keep up with him. He was an ox."

"You're sure."

"I am."

"What are you going to do?"

"I'm writing all this down for you and signing it in front of you. Come back in an hour to watch me sign and date it."

"I will, but what am I supposed to do with it?"

"If I have a sudden, miracle recovery, nothing. If I don't, then you'll have to figure out what to do. I don't mean to dump all this on you but I guess what I'm doing here is getting things off my chest. Maybe you'll decide it's not your problem or it's just me jumping to conclusions. But you've got to admit, Mickey ain't the picture of mental health and he's in trouble now like he always is. He's a foul ball. He don't restrain himself from evil like a normal guy. You have to admit it."

"I can't argue against that, from what I know. Somebody ought to knock him silly."

"He's already there and that's kind of the point…" Karl scrubbed his fingers on his chin. "He's the wrong kind of crazy. I think we need to get at the truth of what really happened. Mickey is about to get locked up for raping Kathleen Dozier. Who knows when he'll get out, but don't you think he ought to stay there? He's capable of anything. He's no weakling, either. I can attest to that."

Eunice couldn't find fault in her brother's reasoning. She nodded once and said as she turned to go, "You can't rely on the Johnsonburg cops or even the state troopers, I guess. Did they even try or care?" She went to her room to do some homework. The house was quiet except for Connor who had come home, made himself tea and sat listening to Benny Goodman on the big RCA. About an hour later she closed her math book and went back to Karl's room. When she knocked she heard Karl blow his nose and after nearly a minute he said, "Just a minute." There was another quiet pause with only the sound of the radio downstairs, applause and some announcer thanking America for listening, "Goodbye and buy bonds!" Karl said to come in.

When she saw him in the bed he was tossing a handkerchief on his night table which glanced off and onto the floor. Karl had been crying. At first Eunice wanted only to ask if he was ready to have her witness his signature on his statement. She was embarrassed for him and couldn't decide what to say. Attempting to eat up a few awkward moments, she picked up the handkerchief and dropped it on the table, not looking at Karl. Karl saw her clumsiness, going out of her way not to notice his grief. He had to idle his speech motor these days before he could get it in gear enough to say anything. This added to the already long silence that Eunice was desperate to break. "How are you feeling?" she asked and waited.

Karl's tongue was curling up, making his words slur when he finally got them out. "That numbness is back on my whole left side. And I just started to blubber all of a sudden for no reason at all. Just wailing into my pillow. I look around my room and the colors are so bright they give me a headache, and then everything looks like it's melting. Jesus Eunie, am I losing my mind?"

"No Karl. You're just sick and that must be part of it. Are you ok to sign your paper about Mickey Mahoney?" She said the name low and looked at the floor when she did. It was as if it were some forbidden name that one would be punished severely for uttering. There was a shroud of contempt around it.

Karl picked up his writing pad and pen. When he finished signing he looked it over. It contained his three assignments for Eunice on one sheet and the details about their grandfather's drowning incident on the other. He tore the pages off, folded them into a little square all tucked into itself in the childish secret way of folding he and his friends used in the seventh grade for their covert correspondence. He pressed it into her palm somberly. Eunice held it to her chest with both hands. She promised to keep it in a safe place until she decided what to do.

8

THREE G-LADY MISSIONS

Eunice finished her Saturday chores, including splitting logs and burning trash, Karl's duties on a Saturday. The splitting gave her blisters. It was one thirty in the afternoon of December 19, 1943. There would be plenty of time to hike to town and go to work on some of the tasks Karl had requested. It was important to get herself free before seven. She and Karl were excited about the evening ahead. For years they begged their mother to allow them to listen to the Jack Benny radio show on Sunday evenings but she refused, saying that it was not a proper activity for a Sunday. Tonight would be the first of a new broadcast from a local station playing a recorded version of last Sunday's Benny show. She washed up and changed into some more presentable clothes. When she came out of the bathroom Karl shouted through his half-open door, "Is that you, Eunie?"

"Yeah. I was just going to poke my head in your door."

"Can you steady me while I get to the bathroom? It's not one of my better days. I'm just a little shaky." Karl got up from his bed. He stared at the crippled man's toilet with the galvanized bucket beneath it next to his closet door. For a week now this symbol of his decline had become a game piece that he and his mother were moving around. She would place it near his bed and he would awake in the morning and move it, first outside his bedroom door, then into the closet and now just outside the closet door. It was as far from his bed as he could put it but still visible. Verna didn't speak of it once and Karl never complained about it but silently they shuttled it around his room and he vowed to keep moving it as long as he could.

Eunice stood by the bathroom door waiting. She talked through it, telling her brother, "I'm going to the bus station and a few other places to check about the key and I'm meeting Kevin Barry at the library. So with luck I'll have some detective work done by supper." Eunice disguised her eagerness with a flat, bored manner that Karl knew was just poor camouflage.

Karl flung the bathroom door open. A big smile took over the whole of his face and he rubbed his knuckles on her scalp until it burned. "Go get 'em tiger. We'll have a secret meeting after the war news and Jack Benny."

As soon as Eunice got Karl back to his bedroom she ran down the stairs past Verna and swiftly grabbed her coat off the hook by the front door. "Where to in such a hurry?" Verna stood, arms crossed near the kitchen door. "I'm going to the library and to Gorman's for a hot chocolate. I'll be home for dinner."

"I should say so, young lady. I'm making meatloaf and mashed potatoes. We'll have green beans the way you like them and almond cake too. Don't you be late, Eunice Daugherty."

Eunice walked as fast as she could down the muddy road to North Broad Street. It was getting colder and the wind was picking up. When she reached the bus station a light snow began to fall. There were some lockers in the bus station but no numbers on the locks and the engraved trademark said Dexter on them. The train station's locks had no inscriptions at all. She looked at her watch and it was 3:25 already. She ran the three blocks to the library.

Kevin Barry was pushing a cart of books to be reshelved.

"What do you want, you little punk? How's Karl doing?"

"He's having a decent day. We're going to listen to the Jack Benny show after dinner. Karl does a lot of creative stuff to keep busy but the doctor says he needs to rest up. He's got this crazy scavenger hunt that he's working on right now. It's for the Lutheran Youth. He can't go along and hunt for things but they tell him what they find and he figures out what to look for next, you know, with secret hiding places and keys and codes." She took the copy of the coded list from her coat pocket. Kevin studied it for a while, looking up at Eunice every few minutes and furrowing his brow. Finally he said, These words in the middle are not words, they're phone numbers. He held the scrap of paper up to Eunice and pointed to the first entry, WOKIFAT. It's WO5-4328. I noticed down the column that the first two letters are exchanges from Ridgway, Johnsonburg, and... looks like Dubois."

"That's amazing Kevin. That's... How did you do that?"

"I know what I'm doing. The first column looks like Irish to me. I can get a translation for you. But you'll have to wait a day or two. As for the third column I'd have to call in the big guns for that, I think."

"What big guns?"

"My grandpa. See, he knows some Welsh. It looks like it might be Welsh."

"Let's not trouble your grandfather just yet." Eunice looked at her watch. She only had a few minutes left to go to the reference section and find an English/German dictionary. As it was, she would have to run to make it back home in time for dinner. She had planned to stop by the post office to see if she could match the key to the boxes there. There would be no time for that now. She hated the idea that she wouldn't get all of her G-Lady jobs done. Kevin turned his back to her and resumed his shelving duties. He harangued her with his head half-turned, acting like she didn't deserve the time of day like he always did because, secretly, he liked her. "We don't allow vagrants hanging around here. You need to be reading or I'll have to shoo you out of here."

Eunice ignored him and handed him the key. "Do you know what this key is for?" Kevin looked at it and said immediately, "Sure. I got one just like it." He pulled a rabbit's foot out of his pocket with a small ring of keys attached. "See. It's my locker key from the YMCA. The one you got is to a locker on the second floor, right above the gym, see, F-2, floor 2, and it's just four lockers away from mine. It's locker number 23. Tell Karl that his treasure hunt is kind of bush league."

"I'll tell him."

Eunice headed up the stairs to the landing where they put the encyclopedias, almanacs and dictionaries. When she browsed the spines of leather-bound tomes she started feeling pretty satisfied. She dwelt on that satisfaction to the point of losing her focus. Eunice had bragging on her mind. She was silently rehearsing her prideful report to Karl of the day's discoveries. She was on top of things now, using her pretty little head for something besides a hat rack. This rush of self-confidence was colored by something raw and new in her soul. She could tell that Kevin Barry liked her. It made her feel warm all over and took her breath away. Unsure of how she felt about him, she was stuck on this new realization and shocked by it. A boy liked her. An older boy at that. This was something new and unsettling yet not unwelcome. Just strange. How much of her new self-confidence was coming from that? She would decide that later, but for now she was prepared to flaunt her successes before her brother. She would soon show Karl that she was as smart as Kevin and as good as any of his friends. It was true, of course and therefore it wouldn't be boasting. She had accomplished a great deal in a short time that Saturday afternoon. She finally selected the right book, opened it quickly and ran her finger down the page of German entries, *S, Sp, Spr… Sprengkapsel – explosive, detonator, blasting cap.*

Eunice drew in a sudden, deep helping of air. It was like a hole opened up in the library floor and she was sucked down into it, grasping for something to stop her descent. The warming aplomb of a moment before had melted away in an instant leaving her with horrible thoughts. Uncle Sean has blasting caps from Germany! Detonators! A sudden bloom of guilt and foreboding left a dull ache in the pit of her stomach. She could almost see God on a throne atop a cloud with a flowing beard and a boney finger crooked in her direction. She could nearly hear a verse in a rich baritone, "Pride goeth before destruction, and an haughty spirit before a fall." Now her little errand seemed so little like the mysterious game she had wrapped herself up in and more like a witch hunt exposing her flesh and blood as a rat, a dangerous liar, a saboteur.

Eunice slammed the musty dictionary shut and rushed out, leaving it for Kevin to put away. Out in the street, the snowflakes were bigger and fluffier, sticking to her eyelashes and falling down her neck. The wind was whipping at her face and the tears on her cheeks stung. Turning a corner, she slid sideways and was clipped by a high spot in the sidewalk. Eunice went down. She felt a hot spot radiating from her knee. Blood streamed down into her sock. She jumped up and kept running, slower and with a limping stride until she came to the shadowy cube of dark stone that was the front archway of the YMCA. She dug in her pocket for the key and feeling it there, rubbed her finger and thumb nervously over the bow where the hole is punched for a lanyard. What kind of keychain should this one have? she wondered. A lucky charm like Kevin had or -- no, a death's head from the SS, or an iron cross maybe? First there was the shock she got earlier when she translated the German, then the bleeding knee now forgotten. Sean Daugherty was all she could think about now. How could he be so evil? He said he had learned to love this country in no time and that he had already overcome how alien and alone he felt at first and how he thought Americans were all blunt and dull-witted, quick to judge and narrow of heart and mind. Uncivilized cowboys with little thought of how the rest of the world thinks and believes. He told her, ethnocentric, that's the word for it.

As Eunice ran up to the locker room she went back to a conversation her mother had with Sean years ago. She said that he would find out that different people lived in different parts of town, separately from one another. The Italians, the Swedes and the Irish but just let there be a fire or a flood or a bad wreck on the road and they pitch in together and help one another, Catholics, Lutherans, even the one Jewish family we have. All working together any time there's a need. There are good people in every camp. Eunice thought about her mother's choice of words. Good people in every camp. What about the work camps and the train loads of undesirables being shunted off to the frontier to be warehoused in Germany?

She topped the stairs in the Y and ran puffing to the locker room door. Her lungs were sacks of embers. "Anybody in there?" There was no reply, no sound of showers or talking or snapping towels on anyone's backside. She went in and found number 23. Nobody was around. She went back to the doorway to listen for footsteps. There was only the sound of dribbling basketballs from the first floor. She opened the locker and found a cardboard tube with a thin leather strap on one end like the ones her dad sometimes brought home from his plant. This one was green and plain, there was no white stencil of "Elliot" like Connor's had on it. She pulled it out of the locker. Her hands were shaking and her sock felt sticky with blood. Working as if in a fever to get the strap unhooked she couldn't get it loose. Her hands were still stiff from the cold. She worked the leather strap loose as a jubilant shouting rose up from beneath her. She jumped and fumbled the tube, catching it before it hit the wooden bench. She quickly pulled out the end of the blueprint to see Elliot Company, Site 3, Ridgway - Test Chamber. Suddenly there was a loud whistle, then the game stopped and an adult man shouted, "Ok boys, that's it for today." After a mere second she heard a terrific bang. It was the metal gym door slamming the wall at the bottom of the stairs. Immediately after that came the stampeding footfalls of gym shoes on the stairs. She shoved the tube back in and fumbled a bit but managed to get it locked up and bounded out the door.

A red-faced boy with a mass of acne and sweaty black hair reached the top stair and said, "You lost, kid?"

"Nope. I'm looking for someone."

"Yeah? Who?"

"Kevin Barry. Is he here?"

"Kevin works at the library on Saturdays. But it'll be closed in a couple of minutes."

Eunice brushed by him and into the mob of sweaty boys in gym shorts clustered as they were on the top three stairs behind pimple boy. The body smell in the stuffy stairwell made her want to retch. She put a hand over her nose as a path opened up in the pubescent swarm to let her pass. Another boy who looked odd in his beanie and thick glasses held by a strap to his head spoke up. He wore a badly faded Ridgway Elker shirt. The boy shouted after her, "Say, you might want to have somebody look at that knee."

9

THE WORST FIT

Jack Benny played straight man for Mary Livingstone's comedic bit. There was a plug for Jell-O chocolate pudding and Dennis Day told some jokes. The show was running routinely along until Day, who was a famous Irish tenor, took his cue from the program's orchestra and broke into song. Verna was taking her second sheet of cookies out of the oven, the glorious hot smell made Eunice's mouth water. She was enraptured by the patter and preferred Benny's act to what used to be in that Saturday time slot, the Bell Telephone Hour. If Karl was happy with the program change, It didn't show. He looked as if he were in his own world. He chuckled a few times in the opening but now he was still. Maybe the tenor was not his favorite. Connor sat in his great upholstered armchair and Mister Lardner, one of the Sunday School teachers, sat across the coffee table from him. He had settled into that spot an hour earlier, while Verna was mixing the cookie batter. All through the war news Mister Lardner had volunteered his commentary. A self-proclaimed expert on the Book of Revelation, he related the news events to the apocalypse. Truly the end was near, with wars and rumors of war and strange signs in diverse places. Connor was polite and winked his eye, pointing frequently to the RCA Victor's tapestry-covered speaker. From the shocked look on his face Mister Lardner clearly thought the second coming of Christ was nothing to wink at. But he would stay quiet a while until some event or other from the news report sparked a sudden recollection of a critical passage of scripture so relevant to the present day that he was compelled to interject. Verna was the only one who listened to him much. While she baked she popped into the living room a few times, saying how interesting and frightful it all was. "We are in the end times, for sure" and, "oh, I must get the cookies out to cool."

Everyone was quiet now and listening to the comedy and music. Connor lifted his coffee mug, took some and set it down. Each time he did, Mister Lardner drank from his mug and set it down. He was looking off toward the corner of the ceiling and taking in the lilt of Dennis Day's Irish ballad.

Karl had his head down. His chin rested on his shirt collar. Without warning, his arms began to swing wildly like he was being swarmed by a nest of wasps. He struck Eunice with a forearm and she went down. She was too shocked to cry or call out. Karl was growling and convulsing, pink foam ran down his chin. Connor and Mister Lardner jumped to their feet. Mister Lardner's coffee mug spilled with a loud thump on the lamp stand and began to drip on the floor. "Good Lord, the almighty, all powerful God!" he said. Connor put his coffee spoon in Karl's mouth. He held it there on his son's tongue for a few minutes. It seemed like an hour. "What can we do, Dad?" Eunice asked.

"He's calming down again, don't worry. Let's just hold on a minute."

When it was over Karl asked his dad what had happened. He looked over at Mister Lardner who looked as though the Four Horsemen of the Apocalypse had just cantered out of the Daugherty's living room. Verna wrung her hands and dabbed at her tears with a dish towel. She used it to remove the bloody sputum from her son's face while saying, "You should lie down now and rest. I'll bring you up some root beer and a snack. Some cookies. Would you like that?"

"But the program?"

"Mister Benny will be on again next week. You've had a bad day."

Connor tilted Eunice's head back slightly to examine her bruised eye.

Once Karl was out of sight with his mother on the landing, and he had finished looking at Eunice's injury, Connor turned his attention to their guest. These episodes, though they had from the beginning sent shock waves through the placid life of his family, Connor managed to keep himself even and calm. With one eye on Lardner's hysteria he asked, "Eunice, are you alright?"

"I'm fine pop, but Karl…"

"Yeah, did he hurt you?"

"It wasn't anything. I'm going up to see him." Eunice was not worried about getting a black eye. It would heal. She was burning to tell Karl what she had learned that afternoon. As she rushed up the stairs she stumbled twice and had to catch the hand rail. She was ordering the events of her mission in her memory and picking up her pace. Uncle Sean's locker key had taken her to blueprints of the Elliot Company's Ridgway factory. The German gizmo in the wooden box was a detonator! She needed her brother's cool-headed wisdom. With Karl getting worse, time was getting tight. Karl would know what to do. He always knew what to do.

She headed toward the stairwell but made a left turn into the den where she sat down out of sight. Her chair was just behind the multi-pane door designed to be latched into its twin to seal off the room. She sat for a moment, intending to gather herself. The blow she received during Karl's seizure left her ears ringing and, until she started toward the stairs she did not notice the dizzy spell that came with it. She rubbed at the side of her head while her father talked in controlled, soothing tones to Mister Lardner.

The Sunday School teacher trembled, reaching for his hat on

the chair next to him and fumbling like he was blind with fear. Connor Owen Daugherty had to find faith somewhere. His wife had found it in her beliefs but he had to reach deep into his own soul for his. Mister Lardner had always seemed a little extreme, a little too heavenly minded than was practicable here in the world of men. Judging by Lardner's agitation it appeared that he was shaken way beyond what the power of his biblical faith could mitigate. If Connor didn't keep his head while his son's condition gradually declined, the rest of the family would have a worse battle to fight. This was the boy's most severe episode yet.

First Karl had undergone a battery of procedures and tests, including an electroencephalogram and a risky spinal tap. Nothing. The psychiatric exam left the doctors puzzled. He had been given regiments of Dilantin and Phenobarbital to control the seizures. Connor wasn't sure what was coming next and what would be the best option for Karl. He would have to make some hard decisions soon but for now all he had was what was before him in his family's difficult here-and-now. He turned the volume knob on the radio down to a whisper. Then he put a hand on Mister Lardner's shoulder. "My boy is pretty ill Gus, as you can see. But we are looking at some better doctors, down in Pittsburgh maybe, or Philadelphia, or Buffalo."

Mister Lardner suddenly regained command of his faculties and bent down to retrieve his hat. "Doctors?" he said. "Connor you have to open your eyes. From where I stand Karl's problem is not physical. I must be completely honest here. I see all the marks of demonic possession. Issuing forth a guttural and hellish growl and inflicting violence on your daughter like that!" Mister Lardner made two steps toward the front door then turned to Connor with all sincerity and said, "Karl is beyond the best of your doctors. I know some folks in Marionville, they can help him. They are Bible believers, strong in their faith and they have had success with the laying on of hands and casting out demons." Placing his hat on and adjusting it firmly like he were about to step into a gale he said, "If you like, we can meet at the church as soon as I can get them to come. I'm sure that they will come and right away."

Eunice pressed her ear on that den door to the point of pain.

Connor was careful to control himself as bile rose up to his throat and heat rose to the tops of his ears. What a night it was turning out to be! Seeing the Sunday School teacher make his way out was among the few welcome sights of the night. Gus Lardner, who Connor had personally caught peeping through a hole in the wall of the girl's locker room at the high school, this same guy who stole pies from the Junior class bake sale was now condemning Karl. Karl was a church-going kid who had harbored not the slightest ire for anyone, not even for the likes of Mickey Mahoney. This was absolutely the worst time for Gus Lardner's wafer-thin piety. His blather about demons. Lardner the hypocrite. Lardner the nut. Religion sometimes makes fanatics out of everyday people. A tree split by lightning at Twin Lakes killed both of Gus's parents when he was 19. The last things they shared as a family were an argument over religion, some lemonade and some baloney sandwiches. He hasn't been right in the head since. At least that was the local consensus.

Connor struggled to remain neutral toward Gus. If Verna hadn't invited him for cookies and radio programs, he wouldn't be suffering the fool now. Somehow the rapid weighing of these facts calmed Connor down. He relied, as always, on the facts and on the same steady penchant for analysis that got him promoted at the Elliot Company. The kind of reasoning that had served him so well all his life. It didn't make him better than Gus, just calmer, so he resisted giving him the bum's rush out into the cold air of his front porch and shoving his crazy ass down the stairs to the frozen mud. He kept things civil, giving a clement response aloud but expressing his real mind to himself in silence.

"Let's hold off on that, Gus. I don't think we need all that sackcloth and ashes business just yet." (Or ever.)

"You can't afford to wait too long on a thing like this."

"We'll pray about it." (Verna will pray tonight. Just like every other night. I will continue to call long distance and write letters to the best physicians in the tri-state area.)

"Good night, Connor and the Lord's blessings and wisdom on

you and your family."

"Goodnight Gus. Sorry about tonight." (Sorry how you, in your usual fashion, ruined our family time with your apocalyptic lunacy. Don't let our door bruise your delicate hinder parts. Watch those patches of ice on our road, they could mean the devil for you.)

Eunice had heard all of the audible parts, while pushing forth silent epithets of her own. She didn't know it but together her inner thoughts, running parallel with her dad's were a kind of silent Shakespearean chorus. What she had intended to do while hurling invisible slings and arrows from the den was to slip into the kitchen to avoid being caught listening. She was so taken aback; however, that she remained motionless in her chair when Mister Lardner huffed past her. He glanced sideways quickly then focused on the front door, rushing toward it like it meant his own deliverance, like a rabbit half a length ahead of a pack of hounds, he bolted and said, "Good night Eunice."

Eunice made no response that the Sunday School master could hear. He didn't linger. Eunice's unutterable reply was: (My brother was the scripture verse memory champion of 1941 and when your sister had her appendix out he had to put on snowshoes to bring her a casserole dish and some pie. Demons my eye.)

Connor came around the living room archway. He poked his head into the den so he could withdraw quickly if there was to be any more awkwardness in this evening. He had seen enough of that. "You heard that, didn't you?"

She nodded. "I think Mister Lardner is full of crap, Dad."

"Well, full of crap or no, if I know Gus his spiritual discernment will be all over town by this time tomorrow night. That's just fantastic. And it's all we need right now." Connor looked at the woodwork above the door as though something was inscribed there that would bring some sense to their evening. Then he reached a hand out to Eunice's shoulder. He gave it a gentle squeeze. "I brought home your favorite root beer and ice cream.

Why not come to the kitchen with me while I make us some floats."

Eunice went to bed frustrated and confused. She didn't get her chance to talk to Karl. Karl went right to sleep and slept for a solid thirteen hours. He couldn't talk but he was terrified. On his pad he had written several lines of gibberish, the only coherent part of which was a single sentence in scrawling script that ran crooked and contained letters of different sizes. It was difficult to make out but in time Verna and Connor deciphered it. *The milkman pointed his rifle through my window and said he wanted to kill me.*

It was at breakfast the next morning before church when Eunice heard of the note her brother wrote. Two things became very clear. Karl would not be in any position to help her now, maybe never. And, she needed to have a conversation with Sean and soon.

10

IN THE COMPANY OF DEVILS

It was the first week of March, late morning on Sunday. Karl was confined to his bed and Connor stayed home from church to look after him. The stale root beer float, with pathetic rusty foam was still on his night table untouched. That dreadful portable toilet was a foot away from Karl's bed where it would remain. He sat up with three pillows between him and the headboard of his bed. He said nothing and stared at his bedroom window. He would remain in this trance-like state for days.

Verna and Eunice were on their way home from the Sunday service. They drove past the Pennsy Restaurant. Eunice said, "Let's take some lunch home for the boys." Verna was somber and terse. Church had done nothing to cheer her up. "Not today," she said. Her heart was down and her head was full of Karl and the tough decisions the family would have to make. The cost of his long term care at the North Warren mental facility was also on her mind. The expense was not really the problem. Her boy would be nearly forty-five miles away and in the care of complete strangers who have dozens of people to care for. Sadness would be her new way and take-out food would be a luxury for the

Daugherty's for a good long time. As they crossed the tracks on the road that passed the Pennsylvania Railroad station on one side and the Pennsy on the other, Eunice looked back through the car's rear window. She caught a glimpse of Sean Daugherty politely holding the door open for Gus Lardner and three others to enter.

The Lardner party took a corner table and Sean seated himself next to a stranger at the lunch counter. The man was well dressed and well groomed. He was gray in the temples and had a red woolen scarf draped on his shoulders. Sean made small talk as if he didn't know the man. But he did. He had seen his green and white truck in the parking lot and sought him out that morning. The last time they had met was in the Summer at the Clearfield Fair.

Sean knew him as Merle Yates but his real name was Schumann. The Schumann family owned several distilleries and textile mills in Wales and Germany. Merle lived in Wales with his mother and two sisters until his late twenties. When hostilities heated up in Europe his family lost their Welsh holdings and Schumann was looking through his crystal at the ambition and nerve of the Nazi Party. Though he was not enamored of their policies, he had thrown his lot in with them. His prosperity was in the hands of a pack of rabid dogs. He had no control over that. First, prohibition then government regulations had kept his distilleries out of the U.S. and, like so many others in Europe he had little faith in American intervention. He was recruited for his spy work by his friend and Oxford classmate, Hans Pfister.

As Sean seated himself at the counter, the two men exchanged nods and smiles. "Is anyone sitting here? Sean asked. In perfect English and a Welsh accent the man replied, "Just you sir if you like. Please be my guest." Sean browsed the front pages of a Ridgway Record as Yates watched the waitress move toward him from the opposite end of the counter refreshing the coffees.

Behind them Gus Lardner was holding court with his three friends. "The boy lives in town here. Terrible case. The demon twists his body up. He growls like a wolf and flails around on the floor there. I saw him attack his own younger sister in their home.

The girl is alright but she has been frightened out of her wits. The entire family is under siege, it may be many demons, not just the one." A thin, severe-looking gray-haired woman sitting across from him sipped orange juice and said, "Don't worry, Brother Gus. One or legion is no match for the power of prayer and the laying on of hands. The Lord of the Light has more power than the Prince of Darkness." There were several amens at the table. Yates whispered, "It seems as though there's war of a different sort in these hills." Sean looked straight ahead and bit his lip.

When Sean received his coffee he placed his napkin between his cup and saucer. This was his signal to Yates that he needed to have a lengthy conversation with him privately. They could not talk in the diner so when Sean left, Yates would follow in a few minutes. These two men were from different worlds. The Schumann family were aristocrats and industrialists. Sean was a carpenter's son from Armaugh in Northern Ireland. Their association in Ridgway, Pennsylvania was the offshoot of a tangle of connections in the UK, Germany, and the U.S. A network that makes sense only in relation to certain events that took place in Ireland in 1939.

Many of Sean's school friends were sons of members of the Irish Republican Army. When they graduated or dropped out of school they joined their ranks. Sean was the only protestant among them, though for the young ones this difference was more the fodder of jokes than a real stumbling block. He kept his resentment in check when he thought he should have been given better opportunities to serve the cause. For example, his role in their most successful raid was mostly logistics and supply. He was assigned to look after his close friend Stephen Hayes who had driven his truck full of plunder to a remote patch of sheep grazing land outside of Armaugh.

In the mid 1930's an American organization called Clan na Gael shipped thirty-five crates of Thompson machine guns to their brothers in Northern Ireland. The arms shipment was an invaluable asset for resistance forces who were underground working intently to get the English out of Ireland for good. One problem the Anti-Treaty IRA fighters faced was that they did not receive any .45 caliber ammunition for the guns. Bullets of this type were very difficult to obtain in Europe. They were too proud to ask their Clan na Gael friends to ship them some, but that all became moot when, in 1936, the FBI shut down the core of Clan na Gael, arresting virtually all of its lieutenants for possession and transport of illegal weapons, bootleg liquor, and explosives.

In 1939 the IRA was flagging. Churchill's men had outwitted the Anti-Treaty forces at nearly every turn. All of their significant operations were stillborn. Prosecution and jail had become part of doing IRA business. England had the best covert organization in the world. They enjoyed committed cooperation from the Special Branch of the Irish National Police. Any edge the IRA had enjoyed in recent years was severely blunted. The leader of a fringe group called Clan na Casúr (Clan of the Hammer), Felan "Tom" Donleavy was seeking a triumph to restore the IRA's morale. He organized a raid on a Dublin armory scheduled for Christmas 1939 just four months before the Nazis invaded Poland. His target was a very large cache of tommy gun ammunition. The haul was over a million rounds, a dozen more crates of the submachine guns and, oddly, several cases of swords. Donleavy knew that the war was coming when he proposed his plan because he was himself a Nazi operative, code named V-Held, which means Agent Hero. He was working with an asset in Germany who, contrary to most of his contemporaries had not lost faith in the effectiveness of Tom Donleavy's group. That contact was Doctor Hans Pfister.

Donleavy's team struck on Christmas Eve when the armory was understaffed and not at their best. The Brits had been raising toasts all night inside the armory compound. When the Clan na Casúr men and IRA soldiers rang the bell at their gate at midnight to deliver a gift-wrapped box, they stormed the place and exited quickly with fifteen truckloads of military weaponry and ammo. Sean had been with Clan na Casúr for a year. He was 18. Tom Donleavy had taken to the boy and got him some training in explosives and hand-to-hand combat. It was Donleavy who told Sean that he wasn't ready to take part directly in the Christmas raid but he would be taking care of his school chum, Stephen Hayes instead.

*   *   *

In Ridgway after Sean met with Yates, the Welshman left the Pennsy, stood outside the front door and pulled on a pair of kid gloves. He watched Sean pull his pickup out of the lot and drive out north toward Johnsonburg. Outside of town Sean slowed to thirty miles an hour waiting for Yates to catch up to him. They both exited the highway to the left into a tunnel of half frozen tree branches leading to a crescent of dirt and rock on the bank of the Clarion River.

Yates reached into his inside coat pocket and removed a silver flask. He handed it to Sean who threw it back without ceremony. "A nice bracer for this cold afternoon."

"What is it?"

"Some very fine brandy that my family makes. Most people can't afford it. What brings us to the riverside today, fishing? I would hope for an update on your project."

"Things are in motion for that. The device is assembled and the plan is being finalized to plant it. The problem is, when I agreed to do this job I didn't know what the target was. Are you aware that my brother is employed at the Elliot Company?"

"Yes," Yates sat flatly. He engaged in some theater for Sean's benefit. He nodded solemnly and cast his eyes down to the frosted soil. He could tell what was coming next and wanted to look as sympathetic as possible. "I understand your trepidation but I'm sure we can arrive at a solution."

"Do you understand loyalty, family? Do you understand blood, Mister Yates?"

"Yes and there has been a lot of blood. I consider Germany as my home now and in Germany there has been too much blood."

"I mean the blood that runs through my veins. Same as Connor Daugherty's, and his wife and children's veins too."

Yates's face grew stony again, and stern. The soft and fatherly tone was gone. His voice was no louder than a whisper, raspy and forceful. He drank from the flask and offered more to Sean. "You should take another bit of this for strength to hear what I'm about to impart to you, my young friend."

Sean pulled on the silver flask long and hard. He started to return it to Yates's hand but took a second drink first. "Hear me out first. You can tell Doctor Pfister and your favorite muscle men or anyone else you like but I don't fuck my friends over and I certainly don't do it to my own brother."

"This can be handled without harm to your brother."

"I don't see how. And I'm not through. When I was taking care of Stephen Hayes after the Christmas raid he acted shamefully and he played the cad. I took good care of him. Risked my own skin doing it. I got him the best food and drink, even firewood and coal. I took Maureen O'Duffy out to the shepherd's barn we put him up in. She acted shamefully as well. She went back without me and she slept with him. She was my girl, Merle, for more than a year."

"That's most unfortunate, Sean but I don't see what…"

"We were to be married. But I'm glad I saw her colors when I did. In any case, I knew from the way they were acting that they had been at it. I never let that get in the way of the mission. When it was all over I might have had to settle things with Stephen but Irish Intelligence took care of that for me. He went down with the fine English pistol I got for him. Fine as the brandy you make. Maureen got picked up by the Royal Ulster Constabulary. Afterwards she started seeing the sergeant, Dennis O'Donnell, is his name. And a fine figure of an asshole policeman he is, if ever you saw one. Three or four Saturday nights in a row O'Donnell enjoyed Maureen's company which would continue as long as he kept quiet about Stephen's whereabouts. Or rather, until Irish Intelligence put it all together. Like lightning they hit. I was on my way to the barn to warn Stephen, maybe take up a gun with him but when I came over the hill into the woods I saw these goons coming for him. They smoked him out with gas and they shot him like a dog. Maureen was never seen again."

Yates stepped back and a patch of ice under his boot heel crunched and snapped. Both men looked down at the cloudy white heel-shaped hole with brown earth revealed under it. Sean said, "Be careful, Merle." He reached for Yates's elbow to steady him. Yates smiled and grasped Sean's forearm. "There's no danger here. But, my friend, we have seen plenty of suffering. We have had to make compromises. As far as the girl goes, there are other women. Your young Miss Cleo Armstrong, for one." Sean was unaware until that moment that his movements were being monitored. Yates continued, "There is so much evil in our world. Take Hitler. When we get Germany back on her feet, Wales and Ireland will prosper too. You watch and see. I have had many a discussion with Doctor Pfister, we will be rid of Der Fuhrer easily enough. The lunatic... pig."

"But what of my brother's prosperity? What of his family, his life?"

"I understood that your plan was for detonation during the night shift. This will work out, I am sure." Yates extended his flask again to Sean. "Here son, for strength. And drink to the future. You must know, you are a smart, capable young man, that is why Donleavy sent you here, and why you have Herr Doctor Pfister's blessing too."

Sean was still reeling from Yates's deliberate revelation about Cleo Armstrong. He would have preferred to knock that flask to the ground and spit in his face. Instead he lifted the silver vessel to the sun as the clouds parted and a bright flash struck the window of his truck. "To the future. And to Connor Daugherty." He screwed the top back on the flask. Inside he knew that Donleavy, Pfister, Merle Yates or whatever his name really was, not a single one of them cared a wit about the Daughertys. Yates did not return the toast, he slipped the flask back into his pocket. Sean felt a piercing feeling, a realization that he had likely just made a fatal blunder showing his doubt to his fellow saboteur. He was in the company of devils and he would be devoured.

11

WHAT SECRET?

When Yates drove away from the river bank, he stopped his truck where the road bent into a hard right turn amid frozen trees. He was twenty yards away and looking directly at Sean. Sean could make out the man's square jaw and bushy sideburns. He held a meerschaum pipe and tobacco pouch. The truck window was rolled up tight. Yates set his tobacco pouch down and reached for the window crank. After a long moment he simply looked expressionless at Sean. Then he nodded with his lips tight and his eyes narrowed. It was a statement without sound and pregnant with foreboding. Sean supplied his own narration to Yates's parting. *You know what you have to do and God help you if you don't.*

Yates was gone. Sean cleared the frost from a stump and sat on it. The river sent velvet sounds to him from a half pipe of tree branches and rock. The sound was soothing and sure. It never deviated. It was part of something beautiful about the country. Sean realized that he never wanted to leave Elk County. He would be buried here but not too soon if he could help it. One thing was sure. There would be no explosion at his brother's submarine engine factory. There would be no rush to a dozen or more funerals and so much mourning. He would see to that. He sat and thought about what he would do next. He would go to Connor and tell him everything. Then the cards would fall as they may. Imprisonment, a death sentence. Connor might knock him to the floor. He was ready for whatever happened. His days of terror and fighting were over.

The river babbled and sang. He thought he could hear words in the rippling water, far away and filtered through the trees, telling him that this was his day to put everything right and face the end of a road that began with his wild friends in Ireland with their bitter struggles and their endless fight in the shadows. He didn't belong with them, though there was a time when he thought they were all he had, and that belonging was worth shaming his own family, living apart from them and the things they valued. He had not understood betrayal until now. He couldn't be part of it anymore. He wouldn't be. A chill came over him, as much from the winter wind as from his reckoning in all its finality and heartlessness. He wanted to be bitter like his rebel friends but there was nothing real behind it. He had no faceless Unionists or Englishmen to blame. Sean Daugherty put himself in this enigma and if there was to be no escape, so be it. He had seen other men go down for not keeping their word to Donleavy. Better him than a lot of men whose faces he sees in the streets, in the bars and diners with their wives and kids. Why should they be sacrificed?

With that he swung himself into his old truck. The starter was stubborn in the cold and sounded a complaint as he pushed the button down. He muttered under his breath, "I'm making a new start, why can't you?"

The spot where Sean had met with Merle Yates was no more than a mile and a quarter from the Daugherty family home near Whistletown. He walked up Whistletown Road until he reached a wooded lane that branched to the right half way up the hill. He heard two shotgun blasts and walked down the side road about fifty yards. There he could see Eunice reloading a double barrel. "Uncle Sean, are you headed up to the house?"

"I am. I've some business with your father. Is he home?"

"Yeah he's getting ready for a trip." Eunice was a little short with her clipped responses. There was a tightness around her eyes and mouth. Sean found the tension as tangible as an ice storm. He assumed that like many young girls she was upset about something or mad at someone and he had caught her at a bad time. But then there was a lot of bad day being spread around for everyone. Normally he would have winked at her mood and left her to it. In a short time, whatever the crisis, things would return to normal. He had to ask her about it. "What's troubling you, Eunice?"

"Well. This is as good a time as any. Let's walk back and we'll forget about the rabbits. I can't hit one today anyway." She broke the breach open and took out her shells. It's too damn cold." She stopped short of crossing onto Whistletown Road and squared up with her uncle. "Sean Daugherty, what business do you have with German blasting caps and coded messages and floor plans of The Elliot Company?"

Sean stopped suddenly and nearly lost his footing in the rutted road. He steadied himself with her shoulder and laughed in a nervous, self-conscious way. When he looked Eunice in the eye, she looked like someone had robbed and beaten her on the road. She huffed and scraped a boot across some rocks. She was ready to scrap (and with a shotgun in her hands too.) "I'm thinking I have no business with that stuff at all," he said, "which is the very thing I want to discuss with Connor. Hell, I was involved... how on God's green earth did you come to know about these things, and asking me, now, today of all days?" He was no longer addressing Eunice but staring at the scar of a man-made trail the road cut into that mountain. He didn't expect an answer but she gave him one anyway. "Don't concern yourself with that. I want answers and I want them now. What is your explanation, Sean Daugherty? We will begin with that." Sean had never seen this side of Eunice. He was stunned as though sucker-punched but he held no rancor. He loved this Eunice even more. He put that aside and began to unfold the story of his work with Clan na Casúr and the expectations placed on him to fulfill the wishes of the group's leader. The Elliot Company job would be done in a matter of days. Yates had made things pretty clear. Sean couldn't protect Connor. Doctor Pfister must have insisted that the project team and the chief engineer had to go, not just the plant and the engine. He cursed the coded message and the key and the rest of the whole dreadful mess.

Eunice told her uncle, "I was about to learn most of what the coded list is about."

"I can save you some trouble. It's a list of four sort of code names in Irish down one column…"

Eunice interrupted him, "The next is their phone numbers. What about the Welsh list? The right column?"

"The Welsh list it is. You are a remarkable young woman! That would be the corresponding tactical function of each man on the list. My own title is the first, Mix Wizard, then my number at the hotel, then my function quite simply in Welsh, *Bomb Builder*. The man I got that coded laundry slip from has done this kind of thing before, as have the others. In the South Portland Shipyard." Sean's words were carefully chosen and clearly spoken. He looked at his niece's face as he spoke. He saw something he would never have expected. It was her smile, a wry looking smile, as if to say, "I had you figured out."

Sean was wrong in the way he judged that smile. Moments later he began to see his error. Eunice's combat face had softened. Her hand gently rubbed his shoulder. She warmed up to him again and, as his better, silently encouraged him to go on. "Eunice, your uncle is a man at odds with himself, and who has just recently become keenly aware of that fact. It's when I look at my old life. I can't imagine what I was thinking, why I allied myself with these people. My past belongs to another man. One who I can't say I like very much. I'm tired, Eunice, tired of this life." Sean stopped in the road and turned Eunice's shoulders in line with his own. "I've watched you grow up in the couple of years I've been here. I hope to be around long enough to do the same but I need time to think and I need help. I don't know where this help will come from or if it will come at all."

"Let's have no more talk about your not being around. I guess we will just have to find that help. I already thought some of this through. We have to go to the authorities. When I get back from Philadelphia I will have some news."

Sean made no reply except a gesture of resignation. He held two open palms out in front of him, bowed his head for a second and continued up the hill.

Eunice had hunted with her uncle. They had game feasts and card games and many, many good times together. He was very much a part of the backdrop of her life, the strong threads of memory that bound her to her family. She met Cleo Armstrong one day when the couple stopped by the house on their way to the woodsman's carnival. Eunice took Sean aside and gave him her approval. He laughed at her that day but suddenly sobered to say, "That is a treasure to me, gem beag. I mean that." She smiled every time he called her that. It means little gem. Now she had made her decision about the man's fate and with it a judgment of his state of mind. He had been so flip about not being alive long enough to enjoy adulthood because he was scared. A man who is that threatened believes his life is worth saving. She was determined to do that.

Eunice was feeling ten pounds lighter. She had not intended to reveal her plan to turn him in, though she had decided days ago to do so. Her betrayal weighed heavily on her. It was equal parts selfishness and doubt that caused her to keep it from him. A lie of omission. A sin? She wasn't sure. She thought that he would run if he knew her plans. That all melted away the moment he said "I'm tired." Everything crystallized at that powerful moment. Before they went into the house she said, "Whatever you had planned to say to Dad, I'm asking you to wait. Wait a few days until we come back from our trip and see if you still want to have that talk with him."

Sean stilled himself with a deep sigh and said, "Alright. It'll pain me some because I had hoped for a release today, you know, getting all of this off my mind and out of my heart. But I have you for a friend and that helps. I'll wait."

12

AN ACT OF FAITH

Eunice sat on the porch and pulled off her boots. Sean let himself in the front door. Inside, he was greeted by the smell of fresh bread. Verna was on her knees scrubbing the inside of the refrigerator. Connor had his back to the door working on a stack of bowls and jars with a brush. He had a trash can next to him where he had dumped the contents of the containers he was washing. Verna said, "Hello Sean. So glad you came by." She rose to greet him as he walked over to her. Connor turned and bumped the trash can nearly tipping it to the floor. He said, "What have you been up to, brother?" He was trying to mask his weariness. There was a forced cordial manner there. "Grab a dish towel or see what Verna needs over there."

"Oh, Connor. We don't put our guests to work. Sean, we have lemonade and almond cake. Help yourself to some." She hugged Sean and got the pitcher out for him.

"It's not a guest. It's Sean." Whatever was on Connor's mind was losing its grip on him. He didn't look so stiff. Sean could read his brother well. He had hesitated to say much at first. He could see that the two of them were busy. He poured himself a lemonade and started drying Mason jars. "Eunie tells me you are taking Karl to the big city. Will he be seeing a specialist, then?"

"He will. A Doctor Wingate. I wrote him and his letter came yesterday. He comes highly recommended. He asked our permission to have Karl studied by two others too. What harm could come of it?"

"Three heads are better than one, I suppose. I'm glad to hear that the boy will be getting such good care." He picked up the pitcher. "Lemonade?"

"No, I thought I would wait until that bread is baked." He looked down to where his hands were plunged into the suds. "If Karl were down here he'd butter up and eat half a loaf himself."

"Still doing poorly, is he?"

"I'm afraid so. It's awful tough. Awful tough."

Eunice came in with her boots in hand, padding across the kitchen floor in her hunting socks. "I just put my shells in the box and here comes a damn rabbit. Across the driveway. And Mister Lardner with two others are walking up the driveway. They kicked that rabbit out of the brush. Were we expecting company, Mom?"

"Mind your language, Eunice. You're not a sailor. Yes, I told Gus to come by with his friends after church. They want to pray over Karl." Each of Verna's words became quieter than the one before it. Praying over Karl, as she had put it was not Gus's intention. Gus Lardner and his two friends asked Verna if they could come by and cast the demon out of her son. Gus had called it a full-blown exorcism. Verna thought it was just so much hokum herself, but Karl was so bad, she thought he would never be well again. When things go this wrong you reach for anything you can. Anything. Karl had sunk so far that it was taking a toll on everyone. Verna wore her desperation worse than the rest of the Daughertys. After church Gus had called her over to meet his two friends and propose that she accept their spiritual intervention. He called them prayer warriors. They looked so poor and ordinary standing beside their rusty automobile. She hesitated but then she just nodded to them.

That old car, if Connor had seen it, she thought, he would have said, "I wouldn't drive that junk across the street, much less all the way from Marionville." She imagined him saying that with a wide sweep of his arm. Lately there were precious few grand sweeping gestures. Lately, he hasn't had much to say at all. He would normally be going on about the testing of his new motor. It was the most powerful one yet, and bigger and better than the train engines they were making. It was quiet as a whisper. The ideal submarine engine. He hardly mentioned it. She took off her apron and fluffed her hair, looking toward the front door and feeling a steady build-up of mounting nerves. Connor will be furious when he learns the purpose of this visit.

The three church folks were a few feet from the thicket of trees at the edge of the yard. They stood in the middle of the dirt road. Verna parted the curtains to see what was keeping them. She made no mention of them or why they might be stopping there. She gave the back of Connor's head a nervous look. Sean stood drying a jar. His hand was stuck in it. He worked it loose, pretending not to pick up the tension in the room.

Outside, the Marionville couple were bickering fiercely. The woman, Ida Paine, had begun to complain the moment they parked at the foot of the hill. She slammed the door of their jalopy hard. Gus expected to see the window shatter. "Afraid to take this antique up the hill, Avery? Man of faith. Humph!" Her husband said, "Now Ida, I wouldn't want to put out any money for a tow. We just don't have it to pay. Trusting the Lord is one thing but you got to be practical about things." They walked on and Ida lectured her husband on the courage it takes for spiritual warfare in this world. She asked for some amens from Gus from time to time. He kept quiet but that didn't deter Ida. She stopped at the fork in the road near where Sean had met up with Eunice earlier. She sat on a stump and rubbed at her ankles. "Look at yourself," Avery Paine said, "ankles all swole up. And preaching to me all along this road. Physician, heal thyself."

The Paines' argument reached its pinnacle as the Daugherty house came into view. Avery wouldn't budge. "We can't go through with this today, Gus." Ida gave a loud gasp as if she had just seen a rattler. "Come on you two. We hiked up a mountain in the snow and I plan to see to it that it's not for nothing."

"No Ida. That is my final word on it. This kind needs preparation. We need to go back home and get prayed up better." Ida started toward the house. Avery snatched her arm. She stomped her feet like a spoiled child.

"Avery! Will you listen to reason?"

"This is reason. Divine reason. Now we are going back to the car. We'll get the whole church praying. Then we'll come back. I'm sorry Gus but that is it."

Gus put his head down. He had never seen a person get a devil thrown out of him. Gus loved dramatic events as a rule. At least these fiery folks were giving him a good show. He decided that the two prayer warriors were not the spiritual giants everyone seemed to think they were. Arguing and carrying on. And now this weak excuse of Avery's. He thought he would let them go back home and stay there. It was too bad for Karl that they were just a couple of phonies. Fakers. Hicks. They probably have a box of venomous snakes in their trunk. He wasn't sure yet what he would say to Verna. She would be deeply disappointed.

"Whatever you say, Avery. I'll catch up with you. Just let me talk to Mrs. Daugherty." The Paines started back down the mountain. Ida was limping and grumbling.

Gus made up an excuse that Ida was showing flu symptoms and began to feel feverish. "Don't worry folks. God has a plan for Karl." He hurried out the door.

13

PHILADELPHIA

Sean drove his brother's family to the train station. They carried Karl onto the train and laid him into a berth. Verna took the one beneath it and thanked Sean flatly for all his help. As Connor and Eunice prepared to go to their seats they discussed plans with Sean for the return trip. Verna lay with the curtain pulled and sobbed as quietly as she could. Connor grasped his brother's arm and said in a whisper, "Everything is going to change for Karl now. It depends on what this Doctor Wingate says. I'm trying to see some kind of brightness. There's a chance this Wingate fella will have... something." Eunice couldn't bear to look at the men. Her father's voice began to crack under the weight of his son's condition. All those months and no improvement. She understood in that instant that there were some words he would not allow himself to speak, the ones about the hopelessness, the doctors and their failures. His immeasurable frustration was hers and Verna's too, watching her son shrink to ninety pounds and loose his spark and his beaming light, and to stand by unable to do the smallest thing to make him right again. Connor stopped talking and Eunice looked at the clean but threadbare maroon and taupe carpet. This was her family's definition of hard times. The immense downward pressing of it collected in the back of her throat. She had never before seen her father cry. Every sign of weakness had been miles away from him until today. Eunice stood by quietly, one hand on the back of the seat, it's sturdy solid feel welcome in that moment. She gripped it and waited until her father finished with her uncle.

Sean asked, "How bad is it?" Connor composed himself enough to give him a picture of his son's downward slide. Karl had not eaten for a week. The conscious Karl had paid his family one last visit midway through that week and departed for good. When he did speak, he talked about the way his world looked, melting lamps in bright colors in his room and strange flying dogs with fly eyes swooping through his windows. He told Verna that his father had systematically poisoned him with bad mushrooms and moldy choke cherries and that one of the flying dogs told him that Archie Mahoney and a man named James Picasso were installing a howitzer at the bottom of the hill. The boy's eyes were alight with the terror of the winged dog's account of these two men's plans for shelling the Daughertys. Karl was spitting and crying when he told his mother, "We have to get away right now!" Then he passed out on his bed where he remained, wet with sweat and still as in death. The wild tale of annihilation was the last of Karl's intelligible speech. Connor said, "My God, well, as you can see the boy is the very picture of death itself. I hope our trip has not been planned too late."

"Now Conner, you know you've done everything you could." Sean backed up a step to reach out and hold both of Connor's shoulders as though he might topple into him. A man in uniform came checking for tickets. Sean made another step back and glanced toward the door. Connor covered his face in his hands, "I should have found Wingate sooner. I should have..." Sean shook his head no. "Karl's mind and his body are failing him but you would never fail Karl. Not in any way." The train was about to depart. Sean searched for a comforting word, some lie he might tell them about miracles and medicine. Instead he said, "When you return then, brother." Connor nodded and made his way to his seat. Sean took both of Eunice's hands, "When you return." He pressed her hands. "And take care of your folks."

She said she would and added, "And that other trouble, we will definitely have some things to talk about there too." He was sure they would. They would probably be talking about a lifetime of imprisonment or certain death if he were to be deported. It was as though he had swum upstream all his life and he had been a sucker to do it. It was people like Yates who made him keep swimming; now he was done. The uncertainty, the pejorative undercurrent of meaning Eunice intended was tucked away in his mind. He heard the lilt of her contempt for *that other trouble*, that seeped from her voice. It cut into him. He would forfeit his old uncle years with these kids. Losing something he cherished that much, that was his shame. But his shame was nothing alongside of what the Daugherty family was living through. Under layers of his own despair he felt a strange sense of abandon, a mounting numbness taking over. He was coming unglued. Just yesterday when he sat by the Clarion hearing voices in the fast water, he gave a damn then what the river might be saying. Now he had a single stitch left holding his life together, this incredibly vague hope that Eunice could be his deliverer. He began to see that what he thought was her contempt was her determination to somehow change his fate. She was so young and he had lived close to her girlhood. What real answers could the efforts of a teenage girl possibly produce? It was all swirling in a torrent of uncertainty but it would have to be enough. He shut these things out of his mind out of pride. He would make no moves until his niece returned.

*   *   *

Philadelphia was swarming like a hive.

Eunice gawked out of the window of their taxi. Verna insisted that she carry a small purse and Eunice had balked, protesting that she would lay it down somewhere and walk off without it. A purse was just too new a thing, she told her mother. Verna assured her that there were many, many things soon to become part of her daughter's world.

She had never been in a cab in her life. The big soiled-looking buildings were so imposing, so high. The streets were filthy with litter, oil, soot, the shops jammed together randomly like a patchwork quilt. There was noise and smoke and smells, not all of them good ones.

Connor was again his quiet self. He was confident and in control again as the family folded themselves into this new place for a time. Once in their hotel suite, Verna lay down and quickly went to sleep. Karl sat up and looked around the room for a few minutes. He lay back and stared up at the glass light fixture. Connor took some literature from Dr. Wingate out of a leather bag and read for hours. He underlined passages and made notes. He wrote a list of questions for the doctors. Eunice thumbed through a telephone book and scribbled something on a scrap torn from the hotel stationary. She said, "I'm going to the drugstore for a Coke. You want anything, Karl?" She knew he couldn't answer but she never missed a chance to include him, on the off chance that he might suddenly regain his faculties. He looked at the ornate light suspended from the ceiling. Eunice turned to her father, "You Dad?"

Conner kept his eyes on the medical papers. "No, dear. Stay close now. Be careful and keep your eyes open. It's a big city here. And come right back. Understand?"

"Yeah."

*   *   *

She opened the screen door and it rang a little copper cowbell attached to a blue and white push bar that advertised Tastykake baked goods. She gave the soda jerk a nickel extra for her paper cup of soda. Her dress had two large pockets. One was weighed down with change and the other contained the scrap of hotel note paper bearing the number of the local FBI field office. Her heart pounded relentlessly like a blacksmith working a horseshoe. She set her cup on a metal ledge all dinged and scratched, phone numbers scrawled across it. She wiped off the phone's big black receiver with her hanky.

First a female voice answered and when Eunice described the type of important information she wanted to give the agency the woman said with an accent snapping like humid gusts in Hoboken,

"Hold, would ya hon while I transfer?"

The agent in charge of domestic spying cases was reading the Philadelphia Enquirer. He had his back to a cabinet in his crowded closet of an office. Clement Stanley wore tortoise shell spectacles and a mustache intended to mask his youth. He was twenty-six. A fit young man with sandy hair and an athletic build, Special Agent Stanley had a few pox scars that added an accent to his ruddy good looks. He had piercing blue eyes which, had they not been set in his brow in such an intensely infant-like arrangement, they would be a frightening, probing menace. His clothes were from a rack at Penney's but he wore them well, always neat and meticulous. He dressed smartly and cultivated a studious look. He could well have been a marketing student at Penn. With eyes still on a headline about neighborhood metal and rubber drives he lifted the phone.

"Hello," said a girl's voice. It was an inquiry as much as an introduction.

"This is Special Agent Clement Stanley. What can I do for you Miss?"

"Mister Stanley, thank you for talking to me today. I believe I have a tip for you about… well it's about sabotage."

"That's fine. Would you care to give me your name or do you prefer to be anonymous?"

The agent's trained ear heard Eunice stumbling over this. The FBI man was so matter-of-fact, like he had received a hundred calls like hers. Eunice had never made one remotely like it and suddenly knew that she had taken this leap too quickly. She had not thought this part through. After a hesitation she went on, "Well, uh. How would it be if I gave you some details first and let you know some of what I know? I'm a little scared, not for myself but for my… someone I care about who is in a lot of trouble. I don't know what's going to happen to him. I need to get some idea of his fate before I come out in the open."

"I understand completely. Now, you can call me Clem.

Everyone does, whether I like it or not. Please, go on. Take your time. I have talked to many, many people in exactly your position. Try to relax and let's just talk. You and me."

Eunice had trouble getting started. She and her uncle had a lot at stake. Since the day Karl asked her to snoop around and get into Sean's dealings with international criminals and enemy spies, she was constantly struggling with what to do. If Karl's hunch was right it could go very badly for their uncle. If her brother was wrong (and if he managed to beat his disease) the three of them would have a good laugh and simply go on as if nothing had ever happened. Sean wanted out and she wanted to do right by him. Eunice had intended to take the FBI man's temperature in this first conversation. But Clement Stanley was in control. From the outset, she wanted to remove the uncertainty, but she felt so many different things at once, the fear, the shame and worst of all she began to doubt that this was the right thing to do. Now that the facts were being revealed to a stranger, her mind was racing. The more she tried to sort through her feelings, the more dirty and dishonorable this business looked to her. If she let it go by, many innocent men would be burned to death. There was no glossing it over. She went on cautiously and told Special Agent Stanley about Karl's discovery of the wooden box in Sean's cabin. She was careful to cloak everything that referred to her uncle in ways that would not give him away. There was a short sidebar in her story about Karl's strange illness and how very desperate his condition had apparently become. Karl had already had too many seizures from an infection in his brain. Now, because of his continual fits, the doctors said he had status epilepticus and it was very serious. "Karl must have known he was going to die soon" she said, "that's why he wanted me to solve all these little mysteries he was thinking about." When she reached the part in the story where she had discovered what Sprengkapsel meant she stopped abruptly. There was silence except for the faint murmur of drugstore customers.

"Yes, Miss. Are you still there?"

"I'm still here, sir, but I'm afraid to go much further."

"Why? I assure you from what I have heard so far, that if you are being truthful, and that is advisable, you have no part in this. You will be protected. The criminals you speak of are the worst kind. They have already killed and will kill again, having tasted success elsewhere. It's up to us to work together to see to it that they are stopped."

"Please, Agent Stanley…"

"Clem."

"Clem," she said, fighting back the tears she was so intent on not shedding, "I'm not worried about myself. I care very dearly about the man who owns that wooden box and everything in it. That man has not killed anyone, but, you're right, the others have. In South Portland Maine. The attack on the dock there. The fire that all of the papers said was accidental. But as for my friend, he will be more than willing to cooperate with you. He will make sure these men are caught before they do what they have planned to do next."

"You are going to have to tell me who that man is, your friend with the wooden box. I'll have to meet with him and get a commitment from him to aid me and my colleagues in our investigation."

"I'm afraid I can't tell you that yet. He has a code name. I will refer to him with that for now. Mix Wizard." All this business of codes and fire bombs was dizzying. She felt sedated or drunk. Maybe she could rush back to Ridgway. Maybe she and Sean could change the plan and he could go somewhere far from all of this.

"Alright. For now," Clem said soothingly. "Let me tell you something. We have been following some leads since that business at the shipyard. Six people died, eleven more were very badly burned. They build Victory Ships there but the operation has been set back for a while. If our suspicions are correct, you and Mister Mix Wizard can likely help us close in on them. Is one of them a gentlemanly kind of fellow passing himself off as a Welshman?"

Eunice recalled the column of code in Welsh. "Yes, I believe so." She looked at the wall clock in the drugstore and realized that nearly twenty minutes had passed. "I have to hang up now. I will try to call again later tonight or early tomorrow."

Special Agent Clem Stanly was desperate to keep this young woman talking. "No. Don't hang up yet! I have to..." He heard the distant and rapid click and the line was dead. The lonely dial tone droned on as Clement Stanley held the phone to his ear for a long time, as if holding it there would somehow bring that young voice back. He needed more. His analytical mind was in overdrive. He finally placed the Bakelite receiver back on its switch-hook cradle. Now he heard only the bubbling of the coffee pot and the tick-tock of the office wall clock which was impersonally and mercilessly measuring time. He removed his glasses and rubbed the tiny crow's feet next to his eyes. The special agent wrote his thoughts on a yellow pad he pulled from his pencil drawer. It was his laundry-list method, which had become a fixture throughout his five years of service, two promotions and thirty-five closed cases. On it was every salient characteristic he could glean from his tipster in that short conversation.

Sincere: yes   Strong will: to a point

Holding back: yes   Intelligent: yes

Involved: no   Under threat: if she keeps holding back

Truthful: likely—so far   Character: loyalty/honor

Her source is more than a friend
Does Mix Wizard know she is talking to us?

Clement Stanley reported this breakthrough tip immediately to his superiors. They agreed with his request to arrange a meeting with the caller's "friend," and they agreed to offer amnesty in exchange for information leading to arrests. He had rushed his memo to their desks, smeared typeface and misspelled words and all. No one cared about the shabbiness of it. This was a golden lead. After months of tedium, boredom and dead ends left to them by these conspirators, this telephoned information was Agent Stanley's first major break. The men he was looking for were not amateurs. They had continually stayed a step ahead of the FBI but now one of them was having second thoughts and may become their Judas. Agent Stanley asked for more resources and inquired how much of a deal he could offer Mix Wizard during negotiations. He received the standard answers. "You'll get whatever is needed," and, "It depends on what your subject has done as to how lenient the courts will be. Of course, you're aware of that. But sell it to him. We will find some way to make it worth his while."

*   *   *

The following morning the Daughertys took their son to a five-story building half a block from the famous Liberty Bell. They rode on a street car full of grocery store and restaurant workers, office workers and important looking men with leather briefcases. Eunice kept her eye on the shop windows and read street signs and ads at each stop on the line. They took a short ride followed by a long visit to Dr. Wingate's office.

There were two other doctors from New York and New Jersey working the case with Wingate. The three physicians were clustered by an admittance desk. In the waiting area there was a woman in her twenties who had an odd, drooping on one side of her face. She looked on as the doctors talked. A half hour after they took Karl down a hallway amid six examination rooms, Verna returned to the waiting room and found Eunice chatting with the young woman. They were telling jokes to one another. Eunice's new friend's lips on her bad side made a rapid sucking sound when she laughed, a sound she might have made if she were preparing to blow candles out with one half of her mouth. "I'm glad you are making friends, Eunice. It will help pass the time." Eunice introduced the woman as "Mrs. Alva Ringling, no relation to the circus."

"Nice to meet you. Are you here to see Dr. Wingate?"

"Yes. He is a very fine doctor. I just know he'll help your boy."

Verna smiled weakly and changed the subject. She took three dollars from her purse. "Eunice why don't you kill some time shopping. The doctors are doing a lot of tests and examinations of every kind. It's going to be two hours or more."

Eunice politely parted with Alva Ringling, failing to separate the young woman from some spotlight in a big top in her imagination. Verna and Connor spent most of the following two hours sitting in a conference with the other two doctors in a kind of store room across from where Doctor Wingate was testing reflexes, drawing blood, injecting sulfa and other drugs, and piercing Karl's body in a dozen places with a needle.

Doctor Plotz from New York did most of the talking. There were many questions about the progression of Karl's condition. Plotz was a short, round man with pink skin like a baby's. Connor was sure that he had heard of him. He peeked into his stack of medical papers and found that the doctor had written some of the articles there. Doctor Dunham was from New Jersey and interjected on occasion, "Yes we have seen such symptoms," or, "It is very uncommon so we have so few case studies." He mostly sat and made notes in a leather-bound notebook with his gold pen.

There was only one question for Doctor Dunham. Verna recalled his article in a medical journal from among the collection in Connor's leather bag. She asked him if Karl's problems could have come from his fight with that awful Mahoney boy. Her tears forced themselves into the corners of her eyes. "He seemed normal until that Thanksgiving day."

Dunham fidgeted with his pen. He looked over at Doctor Plotz who said, "If I may, doctor." Dunham nodded and said, "that's fine."

Doctor Plotz continued. He looked to Verna and Connor. "Think back to before that day. Can you think of any different behaviors, speech patterns or anything odd or unusual?"

After a silent time Connor said, "The blanking out he was having, you know..." Verna remembered then. "Yes, that's right, she said, "he would be talking away and suddenly stop like he forgot he was talking. Right in the middle of a sentence. Then he would get up and do something else or start again on the same subject from the beginning. I just thought he was trying to make sure he got the story right. He has always been a very meticulous boy."

Dunham said, "The connection with his head injury is doubtful, Mrs. Daugherty." He looked over at Doctor Plotz again and back to Verna. "We might say that all the blow to his head did was accelerate things a bit. You see, of the eight cases I have studied, only one had a history of any significant head injury. It was a tugboat worker in Atlantic City. His injury had occurred nearly two years before he reported his symptoms." Doctor Plotz referred to a few rare nervous disorders and one case of a young girl who had ingested some toxic plants, cases he had personally observed, cases in which his patients hallucinated, become paranoid and suffered a loss of speech. None of them had the specific paralysis, on one side of their bodies, nor had they suffered the rapid decline they had seen in Karl's case. Two of them recovered. One relapsed and died.

Through the conversation Connor became more and more agitated and stood up at one point, unable to contain his own nerves. He felt sure that someone had turned up the heat in the radiators. His mouth was dry and his brow beaded up with sweat. He clasped his hands tightly to keep them off of the lapels of Plotz's white coat. The two doctors rose and offered their soothing words meant to calm Connor enough to finish their questioning and get to the part where they would offer some hope of an effective new treatment for his son. Connor was growing impatient with the consultation, for him the details he and Verna were asked to recount were like stab wounds. It was all futility. He was sure that there would be no good ending in this story for Karl. When Connor sat down again, Doctor Plotz said, "There is a new theory in the Neurological field that patients who exhibit these kinds of profound problems have a fever in their brains."

Connor and Verna had heard many theories about Karl's malady before but the way this cherubic doctor spoke in his pleasant voice and with such confidence and authority was at least a little heartening for them both. The two besieged parents were allowed an easy breath or two. Karl's rapid decline, and with it their helpless, hopeless and sleepless lives had nearly broken them. The Daughertys had been thoroughly robbed of their hope. Doctor Plotz was reading an unspoken code of longing in their faces. He understood that he could only bring the facts to them, not news of a plan to fix their boy. With a veil carefully pulled over his own sadness he continued with the thing they had feared the most, the disappointing conclusion that he and his community had come to. "If only we could see inside of Karl's skull and test tissue and find a cause. The diagnoses, we think, are as diverse as the stars in the heavens. Everything from mercury poisoning to demonic possession. Currently these cases are too rare and poorly documented, and we have no means of properly examining the site and source of a problem like this. X-Rays give us nothing and probing for a sample creates an all-too-likely lethal result. Never mind that we need to develop effective compounds to halt such infections."

Connor stood again and picked up his bag full of useless paper. He allowed his words to slowly billow out like the steam in the radiator, more like a calm and factual statement than an angry indictment. "So you, all three of you and all your science… you don't know what is wrong with Karl, not really. That is it, is it?"

Doctor Dunham put down his pen and adjusted his reading glasses. "Doctor Wingate is, at this moment, administering phenobarbital to reduce or eliminate the seizures. We will be moving Karl to the hospital for a spinal tap and to get some help with his breathing. Perhaps once the boy is settled in over there, he can…" Dunham was interrupted by a nurse who rushed in and stood face-to-face with Connor. Verna gasped and hid her eyes from the sight of this nurse in her crisp, white uniform with every pleat in place. Verna had seen an unmistakable, unmasked token of dread on the face of this messenger. Her message was: "You should come right now."

The staff tried to revive Karl in a frenzy around the examination table. Connor said. "Let's get him to the hospital! Why did we wait?" The nurse who had come to get the Daughertys from their store room conference looked up at Connor from her lifeless charge and with eyes closed just shook her head.

Several blocks away, Eunice was feeling a strong and inexplicable heaviness which she was certain was because of her mission of the day. She would later learn that she was wrong.

14

MIRABELLA

Osmund was tall, just over six feet. At twenty-nine he already started to gray in his temples. A slender man who his fellow agents called The Pole. As in bean pole. His leather wristwatch band needed an extra hole in it. His mouth looked wider than most and he grinned through straight white teeth, perfect but for a chip out of his incisor filled in with gold. A small but distinct scar under his lower lip formed a J and seemed to widen with his smile. His voice was an uneven mix of refined diction and near comic nasal twang, sometimes like Al Jolson, often like quacking. He had come from Salt Lake City only a few months ago and was assigned to this office because he was an ace with codes and languages and he was clean. His Mormon faith was for him a comfort and strength. Stanley was amazed at his integrity. They were opposites. Stanley got his smarts from dirt, pavement and gritty pathways that Osmund didn't often tread. Clem knew that Oliver chafed at his new partner's success because after three weeks in Philadelphia he told him as much over pastrami sandwiches at a deli on Hog Island. "I've got to tell you honestly that I've been harboring some resentment, Osmund confessed. This work doesn't come easy to me most of the time. I'm three years your senior and until this year I have done only the really dreadfully dull stuff." Osmund gathered himself and leaned his tall frame across the little table. His tie soaked up some of the sweat ring from his glass. "Do I have your forgiveness?" he asked. "Sure thing, Ollie. Let's learn what we can from each other and team up, you know, go out and kick some serious ass." Osmund lifted his iced tea glass to Clem's draft beer. "To serious butt," he toasted.

Since then Agent Stanley had made Osmund a kind of personal hobby. He saw this buttoned-down Einstein as a perfect resource for the days ahead.

Bright sunlight beamed through the office window flecked with fine dust. Osmund had finished reading through some files that he now brought to Agent Stanley's desk. It looked like Oliver Osmund would finally get away from the dreadfully dull.

*   *   *

Eunice was grateful that her subterfuge had been easier to maintain than she had imagined. Her folks were wrapped up in caring for Karl. "They'll take care of him," she thought, "I was just sitting around in the waiting room anyway." She couldn't shake the persistent feeling that something was terribly wrong. She stopped in front of a pawn shop that was not open yet for a few minutes to calm herself. As she passed a few street vendors she steeled her nerve and told herself she would call Agent Stanley right away. She wouldn't put it off until later even though she wanted to. "One thing is certain," she thought, "I have to finish what I started yesterday. I let myself get spooked but I have to give them something. I have to play the G-Lady and play her right."

She found a diner where she ordered coffee and a Danish pastry. She left the pastry and half the coffee on the table in her booth and dialed Clem Stanley's number again. A voice said, "FBI, Special Agent Stanley's desk, Oliver Osmund speaking."

"Mister Osmund, I was hoping to speak to Agent Stanley. It's very important."

"Are you the girl he spoke with last evening?"

"Yes and I promised to get back to him. It's very important."

Osmund had spent most of the night going over the files the FBI had on the group of saboteurs headed by Merle Yates. He picked a name for Clem's anonymous tipster: Mirabella. His mistake was the coarse and familiar tone he was taking with her. He drew different conclusions than Clem for two fundamental reasons: reading people was not Oliver's forte, and everything he knew about Mirabella was second hand. He said, "It's important to him too, doll. Why do you think I'm answering his phone while he's in the john?"

Eunice had not considered that. She was thrown off again, both by hearing a different voice answer and by Agent Osmund's forward use of *doll*. She felt as though some unspoken confidence had been breached. She liked Clem but Osmund left her cold. Osmund had studied the written reports. Paper and ink was woefully incapable of describing her fears and her shame. It contained none of the nuances of her feelings in her previous call in which she had abandoned her plans. What Osmund said next made her sweat and burn with a hot wave of betrayal.

The men's room door swung open. "Well, stay on the line with me. I see he's on his way right now. Don't worry, we've been discussing things. We can help you and your friend."

Osmund cupped his hand on the phone and winked. "It's your young lady caller, Mirabella." Clem took the phone receiver from his partner's hand. He heard nothing on the other end. "Hello who is calling, please?" The silence persisted.

Eunice laid the phone down with a clunk and took her lace hanky from that ridiculous little purse to wipe her tears, rubbing them a little too hard. She had propped up her toughness to this point. Now there were tears. Her imagination was playing little tricks on her. She pictured these two FBI men engaging in lusty talk about her in some smoky back room, during a poker game, maybe with greasy playing cards and half-eaten salami everywhere. Her breathing got quicker and her muscles tightened. She stared down at the telephone. She recalled her brother's voice saying as he had many times, "Eunie, Eunie, don't be going to pieces on me." From the phone's receiver she could hear Clem's distant, hello's and she heard Osmund a bit fainter saying, "Did we lose her?" Then Clem again asking, "Who is it please?"

She picked up the phone. "Oh um, it's Eunice." She had not intended to give her name and wanted to pull it back out of that phone line. She further shocked herself as she heard her own voice say without reluctance, "I'm Eunice Daugherty. From Ridgway Pennsylvania and I have a problem... some very bad trouble," she added, "and I need help." As Eunice sat crying, something had broken loose inside, letting her name spill out and the rest came with it.

Clem broke in abruptly but with an expert sympathy. "I know Eunice, and we're going to help you and Mix Wizard. We're going to help him too. I have a lot of backing from my higher-ups here. "What else do you have for us? We need much more to go on here, you understand, right?"

"I don't know how to go on. I'm scared and I thought this over all night. I made a huge mistake, Clem. It was so wrong of me to do it."

"What? What was it Eunice? You have done everything right, the way we see it. It's probably not as bad as you think, whatever it is." Eunice said nothing. Clem had written in his notes when he first talked to this unknown girl from who knew where: *Character: loyalty/honor*. He knew from her crying that from somewhere deep down she was being truthful and that she was not involved directly in any crimes. These were all his hunches, but now, doubting her innocence was still the cold, clinical, professional way to proceed. Maybe he just wanted her to be clean. Now she was talking about some grave mistake. This could mean that she crossed over into the dark place that the people she was calling him about were from. It gave him a peculiar feeling. He wanted to keep Eunice where she belonged, at a comfortable distance. He was beginning to feel that he needed to have a long talk with himself over this. Keep it cold, he told himself, yet be warm and get answers. It was basic investigating. To break the silence, he jumped to another subject to engage Eunice Daugherty again. "You're here from Ridgway. I've heard of the place but never been there. Do you like it there?"

"I have friends there, and family. It's ok. Nothing like Philly. Man, this place is too much city for me."

"I'm from a small town too. Soldiers Grove Wisconsin. It's a nice place to live if you're a popsicle."

"Soldier's Grove? What's it near?"

"Nothing. It's dairy country. Kind of close to Iowa. Several nice places, like Milwaukee, had a chance to be right next to us but nobody wanted to be next to us." She heard the funny way he said M'waukee. She laughed.

"Why not?"

"It smells like a giant cow's toilet mainly, but also nothing ever happens there and nothing ever will. You know how, places like Niagara, they have their falls, Erie has the canal, and Florida has beaches. We had cows that had to be milked and generally pampered and kept from freezing in a blizzard, that kind of life. One day I just up and milked my last cow and went off to study law enforcement." Clem sighed and changed the topic back to the one he started with. He stopped playing the funny country cow-milking boy. Suddenly he was a serious, almost fatherly man who was no longer talking small but getting to the bone.

"But Eunice, I know you didn't call to talk about cows in a very cold place. You wanted to share a burden of sorts. You want to help us." Osmund raised his eyebrows in approval of Stanley's directness.

Eunice was still hesitant but glad that Agent Stanley had steered her back to the problem. She felt their connection grow stronger when he said *share a burden*. He couldn't possibly know what Karl's discovery meant for their family, nor how deeply she believed that it had become her discovery. She may never know what Karl thinks of the way she handled it, calling the FBI as she did and exposing all of it. That was her way and it may never have been Karl's way but here she was. Clem was asking her to go all the way with this and she was trying to start the flow. Karl's world, Clem's world, even Osmund's – it was the world of men. She had hovered over it so many times, sipping demurely from it through a long straw and savoring it. These men with their sweet kindnesses when it suited them. These men who made decisions that brought shame on their families and turned things upside down. It all seemed so impetuous and unthinking, even selfish and brutish.

By now Special Agent Osmund had picked up an extension line. He joined the conversation. "Eunice. That is a very nice name. This is Ollie Osmund here on the other line. I know a lot about your trouble. I'm on a kind of team with Agent Stanley. Again Miss Daugherty, you can start anywhere in the story you like. We'll just listen. You're doing the right thing, you'll see. Don't worry about Mix Wizard. And your mistake, we all make them. Just get it all off your chest. Talk to us."

Clem said, "He's right. Trust us and we will do everything we can for you and for Mix Wizard."

Eunice's mind cleared a bit. Clem had given her a little respite during which she made a decision for herself. It came to her. She didn't own her uncle's trouble. It would be a small concession to her fealty, a rationalization. She admitted to herself that she had not done what she set out to do. Her failure was nothing to persecute herself about. It wasn't too late to take things in a slightly different direction, one in which she would never have to tell Sean that she had turned him over to the FBI. When they start digging around they will find the people on that laundry slip. Karl would have called her plan an end-around. Some football thing that faked everyone into confusion long enough for the runner to get away. She could escape from any shameful face-off with Sean.

The deep breath she took was audible. Osmund held up crossed fingers to his partner. She began, "I think someone killed my grandfather because of what he knew."

15

WESTERN PEN

E unice had taken her story of backwoods intrigue on an unintended detour. She had the distinct impression that Clem liked her but he was afraid to show it. Maybe in another situation she would give him a chance to change that. This was not the right time. In her first phone call everything fell apart. Now Eunice was beginning to feel like more than an observer in the world of men. She had regained her composure and taken control of her dealings with the FBI. She had spoken for nearly forty uninterrupted minutes about the drowning incident of Karl Lundquist of two years ago and it's connection to her G-Lady assignment. When she was finished, Agents Stanley and Osmund sat with an idle telephone between them in the FBI field office. In minutes she returned to Dr. Wingate's office. She sat quietly with a copy of the Saturday Evening Post magazine. There was a Norman Rockwell painting on its cover depicting a man in a U.S. Army uniform with rosy cheeks seated in a chair. He was being served coffee and donuts by a woman wearing a USO armband. Eunice heard a rustling of fabric near her waiting room chair. When she looked up from the magazine the head nurse asked her to come with her. She knew what was coming.

*　　*　　*

Across town the two Agents had different theories about how well the phone interview had gone. "You go first, Ollie. Where are we now? Was that a waste of our time?"

Osmund hated these questions. They were part of the cost of graduating from a desk to the street. When it came to looking at the motivations of the people he and Clem worked with every day, he did not have as many wins as he did with minutia and trivial knowledge such as where the state's largest steel mill was and its annual tonnage of product. He weighed out the information in his head before he said a word. Clem waited, sharpening a pencil with an office knife he kept in a drawer. Osmund glanced at a pencil sharpener six feet from Clem's chair. "When I work my hands, my brain works better." Clem said. "The interview, Ollie?"

"Aren't you disappointed?" Osmund challenged. A shrug was all he got in response. "I mean, there was suddenly nothing at all about Mix Wizard. Not a word."

"Don't forget, listening means hearing what is left out of someone's story. You are dead center on that score. Think about who this girl is and why she chose to tell us this part of it, this tale of dread from her home town."

"This is torture. You know I'm hopelessly lousy at this kind of thing and you love to stick it in my eye like that pencil there. Give it a twist, you know."

Clem was laughing at his partner's unease. He was such an easy target. Osmund was pretty raw but he had potential. Other agents passed on him when asked to take him on as a partner. Clem put the pencil on his desk blotter and rolled it six inches in Osmund's direction. "You want to get better at this don't you? He rolled the pencil back toward himself. "I'm your best instructor, your mentor. Please go on."

"She's emotional but not excessively. And she's on edge, scared, worried. Some of that anxiety could be from her sick brother and all of that."

"Good. Keep talking."

"But this girl is strong and smart. She's the outdoors type. She thinks for herself and she really cares about her family. She led us to the point of really getting the goods on this gang and then she went sideways on us."

"Did she? I'm not so sure. You can't blame her for wanting the upper hand. She was less prepared yesterday. She thought it over all night and she couldn't bring herself to lay down the breadcrumbs to Mix Wizard. Why?"

Osmund smiled weakly and squirmed in his wooden office chair, which creaked a little under him. He shrugged and sat back defeated. When he saw that giving up was not one of his options he said, "Cold feet."

"That's right. Her toes are practically freezing right now because, you said it not two minutes ago. Eunice Daugherty is protecting family, her cousin, or uncle, or boyfriend and she stopped short of selling him out. Why? Because the guy is either family or as good as family to her. She has a genuine sense of honor. I like her. I want her on my side and that is why I gave her this breathing room. I don't want to crowd her, Ollie. But what's beautiful here is, she gave us more than enough. Unwittingly or otherwise."

"Yeah?"

"Oh yeah, and we will use what we've got. Tomorrow you are going to Western Penitentiary, Bellefonte PA to talk to a mister Michael Mickey Mahoney. His file will be on your desk in a few minutes. I have rented us a couple of rooms at the Bogert Hotel in Ridgway. You should be able to make it over to Ridgway before 8 p. m. There are probably under six thousand people in that little burg. If you get there and I don't know Mix Wizard's real name, birth date, and favorite footwear by then, I'm buying you the best steak I can find. The best liquor too."

"Uh. I do love a good steak but since when did I start drinking liquor?"

"Soon as you lose this bet."

"I haven't lost it yet."

"Nor have you made it yet, either." Clem held out a hand to seal the pact. It was duly authorized and binding. Oliver Osmund, the devout Mormon, understood at that moment that he had just made a grave error. He would lose that bet and be forced to imbibe, the gateway to untold debauchery. The slim consolation was that this would take place on the fringe of the Allegheny Forest. Nobody would ever learn of it. The man had never had as much as a Coke or a cup of coffee. He couldn't help wondering what else he would have to sacrifice at the altar of his law enforcement career. Osmund didn't know it yet but Clement Stanley would push out all of Osmund's boundaries before this case was closed. The fledgling agent woke before dawn and drove to Bellefonte.

The next day Agent Oliver Osmund seated himself across a large green metal table from a young man in prison attire and handcuffs. The convict was shackled by an ankle to a table leg. The man was sweaty and smeared with mud, having come directly to the visiting area from a work detail along a highway south of town. "Mister Michael Mahoney, is that your name?"

"The same," he said, "prisoner number 8713." Mickey was wearing a tortured smirk and a nearly delighted look with eyes wide. There was a rude mark above his left eye and blood on his ear. He swiped his shoulder across the ear. "Who might you be?"

"My name is Oliver. It looks like you got into a little scrape there."

"Uh. This one guard walks with a limp. He came out to the work site along Zion Road where we been putting in bar ditches and said I had an important visitor. He made me do twenty pushups in the mud. When I made some remarks about his family history, he didn't like that. But then I called him Hoppy, he really hates that. First they cuffed me then he cuffed me in the head. I can usually count on that every time he gets the chance. Are you somebody important, Oliver?"

Osmund ignored the question. "The guard has smacked you down before, then?"

"Only every time he gets me out on work detail."

"Maybe you shouldn't provoke him. You should try that."

"You obviously never been inside, Oliver. I have a good reason for that show."

"I'll take your word on that." Osmund was sizing Mickey up. His subject was amused by having someone to talk to. Anyone would do. Anything different from his daily routine was welcome. He was wrong in the head and smiling at all the wrong things. Mentally he was on a different track than the rest of us. Mickey Mahoney made Osmund feel a little queasy. The agent decided to go right to the heart of his inquiry. He removed a large black and white photo from his briefcase and placed it on the table oriented opposite of the prisoner. Before he spun it around to ask whether Mickey could identify the man in the picture, Mickey blurted out, "That's Merle Yates. I did some work for him."

"What sort of work, Mickey?"

"Odd jobs. Gofer work, maintenance on gas wells and trucks."

"Did you drive a company truck for Yates Well Supply?"

"Yeah, that's his company. I drove Mister Yates around some. He is pretty smart but, left to himself in the woods he'd get lost as Little Bo Peep in nothing flat. Or he'd take and put his truck in a ditch. I pulled him out a few times. He was smart from reading books and from going to Oxford and shit, but not from driving a pickup in them woods."

"Did he ever speak to you about Karl Lundquist?"

Mickey rubbed his shoulder against his ear again. He leaned into the edge of the table like he needed to steady himself. His eyes darted around the room. "Who are you Oliver? Who are you with?" and instead of answering Osmund, he asked for a Coke. Without flourish Osmund showed Mickey his badge. "I'm with the FBI." He stood and pushed his chair back. "A Coke you said? Okay Mickey, but after you answer me."

"I was driving. That's all. And I showed Mister Yates where that fishing hole was. I took him out there and I waited for him in the truck. Then I took him to the Bogert over in Ridgway for breakfast. I couldn't eat mine. I didn't kill that old man."

"Thank you Mickey. The truth really will set you free. Don't go anywhere." He smiled at the boy as he turned to get him a bottle of soda. Mickey laughed and leaned back from the edge of the table.

Osmund had sat through thirty or forty interviews with criminals of every ilk but always as a second with Clem or one of the other agents. This one went like none he had ever seen. The unreality and the elation of hitting a home run on his first solo interview left chill bumps on his arms. The kid sold Yates out for six and a half ounces of Coca-Cola! The agent gave a guard a quarter and said, "Bring us a Coke and an orange pop. Wait. Make that two Cokes, I need to try one. That stuff must be good." The guard gave him a peculiar look. He said, "You never had a bottle of Coke before?"

"Nope. Never had. But this is a good day and I'm celebrating."

"Don't overdo it, sporty," said the guard.

Osmund returned with the two little green bottles. They always looked so friendly and alien to him at the same time. What could possibly be evil about sweet, black liquid in a curvaceous bottle? Mickey lifted the bottle with his manacled hands and downed it quickly. Osmund left his untouched. "I'm going to have to ask you to swear out a statement about that incident along the Clarion that you were speaking of in a day or two. Will you do that for us?" Mickey nodded. "In that statement, we are going to want to know everything you know about Merle Yates's association with Karl Lundquist. Let's try to flesh out that part of the story."

"What do I get for my story?" Mickey asked.

"Extra privileges. Some time off your sentence. Maybe both." We'll make it worth it to you. Don't look for miracles. They don't show you eligible for parole... ever, and they locked you up in record time. There are people in high places who don't like you."

"What do you think of me? What kind of guy am I, Oliver?"

Osmund had told Mickey that the truth would set him free. Now he was feeling like a hypocrite. He couldn't tell whether that choice of sanctified words had influenced the boy, just that, if it did, Ollie Osmund was himself invited to be truthful and that was touchy in his here-and-now. He took a long haul of Coca-Cola to give him some time to compose his answer. He took a second and a third. His suspicions were right. There was nothing evil about the pop he drank. Not instantly, anyway. Besides exploding like a delicious liquid sparkler in his mouth it had given him some legitimate-looking stalling time.

Beads of sweat collected on Agent Osmund's upper lip. He kept looking at the door. He craned his neck as though his collar was choking him. The set about distancing himself from the cloud of revulsion and agitation swirling like a swarm of bees around this prisoner. It was beyond his typical reaction in the presence of scum. Osmund's answer finally came. "I like your honesty. You wear it well. And those people in high places will be having conversations with people in even higher places about your personal situation. The more you remember and tell us, the better your situation will become. You have my word on it."

Mickey had his legs spread as far apart as his chains would allow. He was no longer jittery or tense. This was an interviewer's dream. Osmund was thirsty for more of the forbidden fluid. He sipped at it leisurely and asked. "Why would Yates want to kill Mister Lundquist? Kind of a nobody, really. A part-time night watchman at a Curtis Publishing paper mill?"

"The watchman thought they were stealing pipe so he followed them."

"Who was stealing pipe?"

"Nobody ever found out. I think it was a couple of the mill guys. Everybody takes home stuff from that place. Karl Lundquist saw them behind the chipper room at about three o'clock in the morning. They was sitting in a gray '39 Dodge, a two-door Town Coupe back in the alley around two in the morning. They was parked right where a bunch of fittings and lengths of pipe was piled."

"They who?"

"Yates and these two guys from Maine. They was just parked back there having an argument, Merle said. When they finally pulled out from behind the mill that night they went over to Ridgway. Old man Lundquist must have followed them because Merle caught sight of his car later on over by the Elliot Company."

"Okay. Hold that thought. Pardon my interruption." Osmund reached into his leather case and pulled out more photographs. They were from a random kidnapping case solved several months ago. Osmund was testing for truthfulness by showing these portraits. Jailhouse confessors will finger their pet goldfish if they think it will buy them something. "Recognize any of these men?" Mickey did not. Osmund put the photos away and showed him the set containing the suspected saboteurs from Maine. Mickey poked a finger down hard on a picture of a tall, slender and sandy haired man of around forty with bulging rings under his eyes. "Him. I know it's him, he drives that gray Dodge. His name is Gil Hammond. He's the one who started the argument. He told me about Yates wanting to stall on their job and wait until they got more supplies. They was all getting jumpy. Gil was angry at the other guy, too. I don't see his picture here. Marvin Sharp. He's short and round with a little gray on the sides and always has a plug of Red Man in. Brown on his chin. It seems like Sharp didn't hold up his side of things, didn't have the goods and that's what started the ruckus. Yates got steamed and told Gil to pull back in that alley in back of the chipper room."

"That's very helpful. Was anything missing from the mill?"

"Yeah. When old man Lundquist left his post somebody else must have helped themselves. Whoever it was stole pipe that was too long to fit in the Dodge. See, that's why old Karl never said nothing about that night. He wasn't supposed to leave the mill until he clocked out."

"What were Merle Yates and his friends doing at the Elliot Company plant at that hour of the night?"

"He told me not to worry about that. He also said if I said anything to anybody at any time about it, I was going to have an accident like Karl Lundquist had. When it all came out that Karl drowned by accident, I kept quiet. I knew Merle wasn't kidding around. What would you do, Oliver?"

"Hard to say, Mickey. Hard to say. He scared you, didn't he?"

"Shit yeah. I knew he beat up that old man and drowned him. What kind of a man beats up an old man like that? I wasn't going to be next. He gave me a wad of money and said it would help me maintain a healthy silence on the matter. That's exactly how he said it. I ain't said word one till just today, right here, to you."

"Nobody needs to know that you've come forward with this."

"It's all the same to me. Hell, I ain't got the guts to do it myself. If I get out and Merle gets to me or if he gets to me in here. Don't matter. Hoppy won't do it. He hits like a girl."

NUMBER 10 RED WINGS

When Clem Stanley pulled his emergency brake on he looked up at a sign above Main Street in Ridgway. Cliffe's Drugstore. He had learned that the locals pronounce it like *Cliffy's*. It was his first stop after the hotel. What better place to find a friendly clerk who could talk with him about the Daughertys? They had a sick son. He went to a rack of household cleaning items and began to look interested in scouring powder. He had a good view of the front counter where a lady customer was purchasing a broom and some cosmetics. When the customer went out he took a package of mints up to the register. A thin woman in her thirties smiled and asked cheerfully, "Will that be all for you, sir?"

"Well, not exactly." He extended a hand and said, "I'm Willard Carthage. I work for the Rural Mutual Health Insurance Company. I'm replacing our former representative in the area. Retired last month and I'm afraid he didn't leave directions to our client's home."

"Maybe I can help you there. Who is it you are looking for?"

"A Mr. and Mrs. Connor Owen Daugherty. I'm sure they still live in Ridgway and they may be entitled to a large claim. I must speak to them before I leave for Reading or I will have to return next week."

"They live on Whistletown Road. I can make you a little map. But I'm afraid you won't find them at home today. They are away for a week or so."

"Oh my. This was poor planning on my account. Is there anyone else in town who could talk to me? An aunt, or uncle or other close relative?"

"Yes, Connor has a brother. He moved here from Ireland a couple of years ago. He's a nice fella. And the Lundquists in Johnsonburg. Mrs. Daugherty was a Lundquist. Which would you like to see?"

Eunice was protecting a man in her phone interview. That was certain. Her grandfather was dead so that left Clem with this uncle. "Could I trouble you for where I might find Connor's brother?"

"The last I heard about the brother -- Sean is his name -- was that he was building some offices for a lumberman named Beil." The woman busied herself writing directions to Sean's work site down on a scratch pad. She tore the leaf from the pad and gave it to Clem. You can find the Beil lumber mill phone number in the Ridgway phone book if you'd like to call ahead."

Clem was in the doorway folding the directions as he walked. "Thanks Ma'am," he said and was gone.

He drove out through wild and beautiful forest land to Beil's mill in Bennet's Valley. He had to stop near a creek bed to let some wild turkeys past. Ten minutes later Agent Stanley was standing under a ladder at eye level with a pair of Number 10 Red Wing Engineer Work Boots. He looked up and said, "I absolutely hate to interrupt you sir."

"I can talk while I'm nailing. If you're a salesman you should speak to the man I'm working for. You passed the lumber barn to get here. Mr. Beil should be in a room behind the big saw. I'm fairly certain that he is in too."

"No sir, actually I was hoping to talk to a mister Sean Daugherty. Are you Sean Daugherty?"

"I can't say just yet. Does he owe you money?"

"Oh no. That's very funny. Does he owe me money?" Clem added a convincing little laugh to his milquetoast insurance man act. Sean had put his feet on the floor and was eye-to-eye. He left a length of molding above his head, half attached to its new home. The hammer was still in his hand.

"Then it would be me you're looking to find. To what do I owe the pleasure today, sir?"

"I'm Will Carthage. I represent Rural Mutual Insurance."

Sean slipped the hammer into his tool belt and the men shook hands. "Mr. Beil's insurance covers me on this job. Off it I think I'll be alright on my own. Sorry, Will."

"Oh I'm not in sales, Mister Daugherty, I'm in claims." Clem gave Sean his Rural Mutual business card. It was not the Agent's first role as an insurance representative. "My company sent me to take care of a possible payment for young Karl's medical expenses. I must speak with his parents soon and try to take care of these arrangements. As I'm sure you know, it is all so unfortunate and serious, his illness. We are here to help the family. Do you know where they can be reached?"

"They've gone to Philadelphia. Karl is in the care of a Doctor Wingate. Just a moment." Sean bent down and retrieved a scrap of wood. He copied Dr. Wingate's information onto the wooden remnant from a card he had in his wallet. He handed the flat bit of molding scrap to Clem, which Sean had grasped in his left hand along with his open wallet. As the visitor took the piece of wood, Sean could see his car outside. Why would a claims representative for a big insurance company drive a dull sedan, a travelling salesman's car? Why drive out of your way to this tiny burg to see him? Why not call Biel to see if Sean was around first? The cut of the man's clothes, his demeanor, it all looked wrong. He couldn't bring himself to look Will in the eye. He climbed back onto the ladder as Clem took the piece of wood. Clem saw Sean's driver's license in a clear pouch in the wallet. It gave Sean's birth date as August 13, 1920.

"Dr. Wingate, in Philadelphia," Clem recited absently. "Thank you, Mister Daugherty."

"Not at all, Will." Sean was suddenly giving undue attention to a routine piece of molding, rubbing his hand several times across it to examine the tightness of the fit. He wanted to be shut of this studious looking out-of-towner. Now he preferred the company of his craft. Clem had possibly lurked about too long and pressed himself too close. In spite of the tension, Sean made a helpful gesture. "Mister Carthage, if you should need me, I have no phone in my place but I'm here six days a week until I finish up. How long will you be in town?"

"A few more days, I believe."

"Where are you staying?"

"At the Bogert."

"They take messages for me there. I'll leave word with the front desk for you about where I might be found in the evenings. If I can help you in any way…"

"I appreciate that, Mister Daugherty. Karl is lucky to have you for an uncle. Lucky indeed." Clem looked up at the woodwork that Sean was fitting flush against the ceiling. "And you do fine work. Good afternoon."

Just before five that evening Clem pulled his sedan behind the hotel and took a short stroll to the lawn in front of the Elk County courthouse. He looked up at the slate cupola and admired the large golden statue of Lady Justice with her sword gleaming in the evening sun. The maple trees were budding and pigeons roosted in crannies of the ornate building. He sat and read the Ridgway Record until he became restless. Lumber barons had built the town and the facades of the buildings lining its streets were solid and fine, their owners' names and company logos carved into the sandstone and granite on proud display. They were suitably august for the county seat. The stature of these buildings was dwarfish compared to Philly or even the Milwaukee of his boyhood. But they asserted themselves with near overstatement in concretely stubborn durability. It looked like many of the other towns he had driven through that day. Why not walk along and get a close look at it? It would be peaceful way to pass the time and think about his next move. That day he had so handily filled in a critical gap in Eunice's story by meeting Sean. His next task would be to get the details of Osmund's interrogation of Mickey Mahoney. The two agents would have much to talk about over the steak his partner was going to buy him. Meat and sides and a good gloat, followed by top-shelf whiskey from the Bogert Hotel bar. They might even do some more work before bed time.

He rose from his bench just as a cold breeze blew out of the north across the courthouse lawn. Chill wind that blew across the little town and up the same slope of Boot Jack Mountain that he had so fearfully navigated downward earlier, his foot poised over the brake pedal on that precarious hill. Clem looked over his shoulder at the statue atop the courthouse that would, in a few years be destroyed by lightning and replaced with a weather vane.

He walked at a fairly quick pace down North Broad, the tree-covered mountain looming over his right shoulder. Walking through town would help him put flesh on the skeleton of Eunice's version of the events that led him there.

Clement Stanley's kinetic urge was driven as much by unease as by a thoughtful change in location. As soon as he began walking, his restlessness gave way to angst. He had sat alone in the small town square with little to draw his mind away from some matters he didn't care to face. He thought about Agent Osmund, Mister Straitlaced who walked the earth with so much gravity weighing him down. A man with no grasp on the art of relaxation. ("Look who's talking," said a little voice in Clem's head.) He's rigid as a flag pole. He never wavers, yet Clem envied him. Ollie had it good at home. He was deeply loved in that sacred space, with the devotion of a good wife and their two small boys.

Clem had none of that. Instead he had bitter memories of Dorie. It was so long ago and he had no real feelings for anyone since. A few moldering, painful thoughts were what was left. She was pretty and quick. She was oh so smart and great at parties. He didn't notice that they were a bad match. She stooped low to stay with him a few weekends and he understood that she would tire of her little adventure and go back to Upper Darby with its afternoon high teas and its long black Cadillacs. One Sunday he returned early from a case in New Jersey with his surprise flowers and theatre tickets. Clem saw it all again as he walked slowly down the breezy streets, felt the pain in his belly just as he had that Sunday. The sight of the college boy in his sweater and his deck shoes. Their goodbye kiss and his wave to her from his shiny roadster. Clem wished he had been more of a gentleman about it and not pitched her the flowers before she was prepared to catch them in that doorway and let his voice rise an octave as he said, "Goodbye, Doris Cavenaugh. I hope you have a good time with your friend Skippy there." Skippy? Why did Clem go so thoroughly to pieces in these situations? Why did he fall so fast, and hit the ground so hard, and act and speak like someone so inferior to himself? He laughed a tiny laugh and then some more, careful that no passers-by would see him laughing to himself like some fresh new lunatic on the streets of Ridgway.

His pain was gone. He walked faster, changed direction up an alley to its terminus. He passed trash cans and barrels, old kegs and crates. He realized that since Dorie he had been suspended in a frozen cocoon. Now two phone calls from a young girl were tearing away its fibers. Eunice's voice, her way of saying things, her inexplicable warmth and things he could not possibly have known about her; his mind had built them into monuments. Eunice called to tip him and single-handedly loosened up the rusted machinery of Clement Stanley's heart. There was no staid rationality in any of it and nothing befitting a sworn officer of the United States

Government. Clem knew that he should have remained detached and even-handed about Eunice. He scolded himself about it. It was exactly how he should have been with Doris when he let her cheat and lie each time he went out on a case for more than a day or two.

But Eunice was not some debutante on a lark on the rough side of Philadelphia. At least in Clem Stanley's field of monuments to her there was no icon of that sort of woman. No stone idol with a sword dripping his blood. He fought against the flow of that blood as he returned from the alley into North Broad Street. It was like pushing the river that was flowing behind those buildings. The Clarion, the River of Pain. He would let himself feel and think anything he might want to about the girl. He had, after all, come alone to this town and left her behind in Philadelphia, and put all these miles between them only to have the whole thing backfire on him. He now walked around in her town unable to stop thinking about it as the home of some goddess. It was so juvenile and even a little irresponsible but here he was, pawing at these imaginings like a starving dog. In these streets he had fought off his nagging impulse to ask these folks if they knew her and if they would tell him what she was like. Of course that would be going way too far. He mastered his feelings but knew they would come over him again like a swift summer squall. He would see her soon enough and he would keep things just as they should be.

Clem stopped in front of The Limit Pool Rooms on the ground floor of a three-story building. There was a jeweler's shop next to it and across the street, the Smith Brothers Department Store. Smith Brothers was a cough remedy most anywhere else. The quiet was ruptured right then and his view of the Smith Brothers building briefly interrupted by a caravan of three lumber trucks, each carrying capacity loads of twelve-foot logs. Their truck engines paused for downshifts in a trio of staccato moans. He was standing a few feet from where Eunice had put a gash on her knee a few months before. She was on his mind again. "Stay on point," he said to himself. The pieces of Eunice's story didn't quite fit together and he knew enough to be worried. If he ambled around these streets so aimlessly too often or too long, whatever was afoot could lead to a disaster in Ridgway. Bad for the town, and of course, the victims' families, but also bad for the two agents assigned to the little spy ring with coded names and dirty jobs to do. There were at least four men they had to find and Sean Daugherty was the first one to check off of that list.

Clem went into the smoke and din of the pool hall and had a fast look around. It was getting busy with the bustle of factory men and lumber crews quenching their thirst, shooting pool and playing shuffleboard and darts. A homely looking, tall, thin man was removing a cue from the rack, checking it for straightness. He was a crisp dresser. His ruddy companion smashed the rack with a loud crack. Clem had a fleeting impression that the tall guy looked like someone he knew. He couldn't place him. He stood by the doorway tightening his eyelids for a flash of recognition that never came. A rugged looking guy in a tattered baseball warm-up jacket bumped him into a table. He smelled of sawdust and oil. Clem lingered long enough to watch Mister Homely make a difficult rail shot on the number nine ball as his stout friend looked on. The other pool player was his opposite, short, chubby and not so neat. He had tiny brown tobacco rivers at the corners of his mouth. Clem was never fond of cheap cigar smoke so he went back to the streets to make a wide circle covering more than a quarter of town, neighborhoods, businesses, schools and at least three beautiful stone churches. His shoes pinched at his feet and the pace he was walking brought sweat in spite of the 53 degree air. The bell in the courthouse tower rang six when he crossed the square. He had reversed his steps. He retired to a booth in the Bogert restaurant where Oliver Osmond sat waiting.

"Ollie. Welcome to Ridgway. You look chipper. And you're early. This either means things went very well at Western Pen or you butchered the job. Which?"

"Certainly not butchered." Osmund underplayed his answer, preferring to be unemotional about his conquests. "I've got some answers. Mister..." He stopped short as a young waitress appeared next to their booth. Osmund took up his thread with an adjusted angle of discretion, "My client was fairly forthcoming." The waitress smiled and said, "What will you two gents be having?"

Clem was all smiles, partly because he had a hunch that it had been a very fine day for him and his partner, and partly because a well-earned hunger was about to be sated with a steak. Cooked to pink perfection. He said, "My partner here is the man to speak to since he is buying. Go ahead Mister Holstein, tell the lady." Clem studied the fresh young girl in the white blouse, a package of Lucky Strikes tucked into her short chevron sleeve. He liked her kind of smile, which took over her face like a photographer's flash bulb. It was having a similar effect on his own face. "We can talk business later Mister Holstein, but please, talk dinner now. I'll have mine medium rare, of course." Osmund placed his order and the waitress said, "I'll be back in a jiffy with your drinks and get you started with some bread and butter." She hurried away and Clem looked over the lenses of his glasses to watch her exit, as much to assure that she was out of earshot as to enjoy her feminine style of walking and the two vertical seams in her nylons.

Clem spread his napkin on his lap and sipped some ice water. "What did you get from Mickey Mahoney, anything we can use?"

Osmund disrupted the damp blanket he was trying to hold over his triumph. "Jeez," he said, "that kid sang me an aria! Went all confessional." He didn't like the sound of his own enthusiasm so he checked it. This was not a demeanor befitting an FBI investigator. Federal business was somber and serious. He used a detour in his answer to calm down. "Holstein? That's a cover name? Am I Jewish? And why am I paying for dinner? You haven't given me any proof that you got anything. Specifically, your target's shoe style, and so on."

"You don't have to be Jewish. It's a fine Huguenot name. Could be Dutch, Swiss, even Welsh, or English. You are stuck with it though, I booked you in under it. C'mon buddy – Holsteins. The classic-looking black-and-white cow. Thought you might appreciate it since we're having beef. You're too literal. You know that?"

"Ollie Holstein, huh?" He tried on his alias. 'At any rate, let me get back to this afternoon's interview. It was pretty unusual to say the least." Osmund recounted the salient points of his conversation with Mickey. He was particularly proud of the Mahoney boy's confession. He included his own indomitable sense of revulsion, calling it a near-nausea, which he felt throughout the interrogation. He had to look at the grimy oil of Mickey's skin and shake off the crawling sensation overtaking his own. "I felt instantly better when I left the visiting room."

"Yeah. That's what happens in the presence of very creepy fellows. I read his file. Go on."

"Well, I will have some proposals and requests for the DA from Saint Marys who prosecuted Mickey's rape case and will undoubtedly handle his accessory to murder case for the Karl Lundquist murder."

"Sure. You'll want to stall a little. Don't even have Mahoney swear out a statement just yet. Sit on it for a while. We have to wait."

Osmund slumped his shoulders and leaned forward. In a single, fluid motion he swiped a hand down across his eyes into a pinching motion on his nose and clasped the hand into a fist he used to prop up a weary chin. In that brief pause his partner looked over the rim of his glasses, again inviting Osmund's response. Osmund used the silence to look back on the whole of his partnership with Agent Stanley. He weighed the dozen other irregularities he had been forced to play a role in, against the threat of reprimand or agency discipline. He found a little comfort in their apparent immunity. Both agents' records were clean. Osmund looked at Clem's impatient fingers drumming the tabletop and gave a tight little laugh which squeaked out of his clenched jaw. "Alright. I suppose I could slow it down. Can you tell me why?"

"Can and will, my friend. Your investigation confirms my basic suspicions. You see, Ollie, Eunice Daugherty is smarter than we gave her credit for. A little emotional like you say, but not to her discredit." Clem removed his glasses for a moment, looking at his partner with a dim vacancy in his eyes. He returned his glasses to his face and continued. "...But Eunice is a digression here. We know from Mickey's version of things that we can put Merle Yates

131

with the two thugs we know set the fires in Maine. Mickey identified one of them as a Gil Hammond. The other is using the name Melvin Sharp. We can put the three of them at the Elliot Company plant. Elliot is a naval contractor. And you have the same files that I have in which there is precious little dope about what on earth they do."

Clem kept watching his partner for tells. Osmund had just revealed the sense of urgency he was feeling over their sabotage case. He had punctuated it with a pulling on each of his shirt cuffs, his mark of pedantic finality and a hint of indignation. Clem was unmoved. He sat erect and clasped his hands together with both index fingers pointing pistol-like out in front of his chest. "Forgive me for an insulting urge to state the obvious." He paused as their waitress laid steak dinners before the two agents. Clem didn't give her a glance. He was swinging in his brain to a hot big-band tune, Benny Goodman, and he resumed before his waitress retreated. "Your murder case and my sabotage are now inexorably intertwined." His clasped hands illustrated his imagery. The waitress said, "May I get you two darlins anything else for now?"

"No thanks, maybe pie á la mode shortly," said Clem. The waitress turned quickly and returned to the kitchen. Osmund bowed his head for a moment and pulled an incredulous face. He mumbled, "Pie was not part of our deal." Clem hurried to get off of the subject of dessert. "I visited Mix Wizard at his job site a few hours ago and…"

"I assumed that you did. Thus the steaks, right? You think you're such a crackerjack detective."

"I definitely am an excellent detective. Take some notes, will you? I've been in this pleasant and friendly lumberjack's heaven for about half a day and I know volumes about Eunice's friend. Not a friend, exactly but her uncle on her father's side. He's a skilled carpenter and he was born August 13, 1920 somewhere in Ireland. He favors Red Wing Engineer Boots, size 10 I would say, and he's in my pocket as long as we're in town. His name is Sean Daugherty. And, if you were entertaining any notion that he might be involved in the Karl Lundquist case, uh, not in a million years. I would stake my reputation on it. If my dessert upsets you that much, I'll spring for the thirty cents for two apple pies, or do you prefer chocolate or lemon meringue?"

Osmund chose a final ginger ale instead of pastry, content to watch his partner devour a hot slice of apple pie with two scoops of vanilla ice cream. Clem scraped the remainder of bottom pie crust from his dish and said, "Tomorrow I'm going to visit one of the offices of Yates Well Supply, maybe inquire about some pumps or some installment estimates for my brother-in-law's farm in Kittanning. You didn't know my sister lives in Kittanning, did you?"

"Well never mind that you have no sister but I'm sure that you will have a very colorful one when you go to the well supply place. An Olympic swimmer, no, diver perhaps? You will be passing through -- what is it?"

"Well, their main office is in Dubois but they parked an old train caboose on site. It's in Weedville."

"You'll be passing through Weedville doing insurance company business and I would guess that your sister's name will come up."

"It will come up. Something that would make sense to name her if you named your son Willard or, hell, Clement for that matter. Vivian maybe. She married a lapsed Amish fellow from Lancaster who shed his abhoration of machinery when he found out there was vast wealth trapped beneath the soil of their little dairy farm."

"Abhorrence," Osmund said."

"What's that?"

"The word is abhorrence. Abhoration is no English word."

"I happen to like it, Oliver. It should be an English word. But back to my family. Vivian, she helped her husband reconsider. She is delighted that Jeremiah would agree to do some upkeep on the wellhead he bought with his land, since the man milks by hand

and plows behind a horse. You know, Ollie, if you got yourself some imagination, you wouldn't have to be so jealous of mine."

"I've plenty of imagination. And vocabulary. Why can't they just be ordinary people, Clem?"

"Because nobody is ordinary. I'm calling her Vivian for Christ's sake. Let's talk about the two bastards from Eunice's coded list, do you have your copy of the list?"

Osmund drew a folded piece of typing paper from the inside pocket of his suit jacket. "Our two bastards, Cart Driver and Heavy Lifter. I called those phone numbers from the list many times. There was no answer on either line."

"Yes. The two Maine boys, AKA Transportation and Supply, and Violent Acts. Would you like to lay odds that we are going to handcuff these two torpedoes within the week?"

"I'm through with bets for the foreseeable future, Clement."

"Wise man. Don't forget our drink later. May I suggest Crown Royal and ginger? I'll be going to Weedville early in the morning. You will be working on a couple of things. Find out what you can about what is going on with the Daughertys, status of young Karl's condition, all of that. I really want to meet their daughter face to face and the sooner the better. I'll go back to Philadelphia if need be. Meantime, you should look for me here around lunch time so we can compare notes. If you find our two friends from up North, please use utmost discretion." Clem asked to look at Osmund's picture of Gil Hammond. He closed his eyes and recalled in photographic detail the two men he saw that afternoon at The Limit Pool Rooms. He chided himself for not recognizing the tall dandy with bags under his eyes. It looked like they could be arresting them sooner than he thought. "They can't get a whiff that anything is up," Clem said. "I want them comfortably moving around these lovely hills like they don't have a care in the world." He made no mention of his lapse of memory. He said, "Can you do that? Oh, and you should start with the local pool halls."

"Will do. They won't suspect a thing."

"Good." Clem rubbed his belly and pretended to adjust his suspenders to accommodate his new girth. "Now, my initiate, to the hotel bar for a little wreck and ruin. Got your wallet?"

17

MUTED COMMAND

The following day was Saturday, March 14, 1943. The morning paper's top headline said, *Britain Suspends Travel Between Ireland And The UK.* The story said that this measure was taken because the Irish refused to expel Axis-Power diplomats. Also on page one, *Soda Fountain Springs Leak.* The plumbing problem happened during the night and flooded the floor at Cliffe's Drugstore. It was a warm, sunny day with a high of 57 degrees. Osmund sat on a stool at the Bogert's lunch counter next to Rich Gibbs, the editor of the Ridgway Record. Under his cover of a Claims Division Trainee for the Rural Mutual Insurance Company, Osmund struck up some small talk about the Daugherty family. He learned that morning from Mister Gibbs that the Daughertys would be returning from Philadelphia with their deceased son, Karl and funeral arrangements would be one of the first things on their agenda that afternoon. "What a terrible shame," Rich Gibbs said, "He couldn't have been more than eighteen years old. A fine boy, too. They must be devastated." Osmund agreed, they must be, and he ordered black coffee and dry toast. Agent Osmund prayed in tender silence for the sadness of this family he had not yet met. He congratulated himself for his strength of character last night. He stopped after two whiskey drinks and read files in a slightly impaired state until he nodded off to sleep in his room. Osmund was secretly glad he had lost his bet with Clem Stanley. And he understood the value of drink as social leverage, as a strategic tool for undercover work. But that woozy feeling he thought would be so pleasurable had proven one part exhilaration and three parts apprehension, a vulnerable state of surrendered mental faculties. Liquor had, in short, been a disappointment. His skills as an investigator were not. He had picked the newspaper man's brain and already had good information on the Daughertys. And he had not yet left the hotel lunch counter. He had no need for libations, just the forbidden hot black stimulant and the breaking of bread toasted and plain.

It was too early in the day for the pool rooms. Osmund decided to look around near every place you could rent a room or an apartment to try to locate a gray Dodge Town Coupe. This, he believed would kill a few hours. The tedium was beginning to make him nod when he found a gray Dodge parked next to an apartment house across the street from the post office. The car met the description in Mickey Mahoney's prison narrative. The agent sat in his own car for two hours before a woman of about fifty came out and loaded several bundles of clothing into the trunk. He told her that he was in town doing some business for a few days and inquired about the rental rates of the apartments. She said she was the building's superintendent. His gut told him she was being truthful and likely had no connection to any spy nest. He asked her if she was happy with the Dodge and how long she had owned it. Her answer was that it was a good car, the first she ever owned and that she bought it two years ago. Too long ago to have purchased it from Hammond and Sharp. She was either genuine or the best actress in town.

With his search going nowhere, he decided to try a different approach. If Hammond was Transportation and Supply, and Sharp was Violent Acts, the men would be looking for explosives for their dirty trick at the Elliot Company plant. It would have been foolish to drive across four states to Elk County with the supplies. Why had they not obtained them yet? These men were professionals. He needed to think like them. Osmund went to the public library.

Among the lumber cutting businesses, excavators and mining interests who would have stores of dynamite and black powder he found one very intriguing possibility. The Noble Mining Company had closed down their Number 2 mine in Elbon PA in 1939. Osmund was amused to see that the name of the village of Elbon was Noble spelled backward and delighted to see that it was less than nine miles from where he now sat. A classified ad in the Ridgway Record announced a sale of assets from the defunct business, including a narrow-gauge coal shuttle, tools, gas masks, first-aid kits, electrical wiring, the inventory of the Noble Company Store, and explosives. The sale was to be held at a warehouse on Ridgway's west end at three o'clock in the afternoon. Osmund couldn't help wondering who would buy a small train, a carnival? There was no time for mental tangents. If he didn't locate the two skunks he was tracking before three, then the sale would be a must-see event for the two agents. He picked up his notes, returned the newspaper to the periodicals rack and resumed the tedium of checking every lead in Ridgway.

Sean Daugherty passed the nondescript sedan Osmund was driving in the opposite direction on North Broad Street. Agent Osmund had a map from a local brochure listing boarding houses, apartments and single rooms to rent. He was checking them systematically. Sean had an appointment with his grieving brother's family at the train station at 11:15 a.m. They had a coffin to deal with before he took them up the steep climb of Whistletown Road. They waited for a hearse to deliver it to the funeral parlor. Sean said he would go by there later to settle things with the funeral director.

Karl was all they could talk about, how big the funeral would be, how proud they were of him and how much he would be missed in their town. Verna did most of the talking as they rode up Whistletown Road. She recalled every admirable trait her son had, funny things he had said and done. The rest of them listened. She was wobbly when she got out of the car and Connor helped her into the house.

Sean cried with them as they had coffee at the kitchen table.

He felt a little strange asking Connor the question that was burning in his mind all day. "Did you hear anything from a man named Willard Carthage? He is with a firm called…" He took the card from his wallet and gave it to Connor. Sean wished he could have put this off until much later. Health insurance for a dead boy? Sean had his own reasons for asking about it, making him a selfish cad in the midst of the Daugherty grieving. "Rural Mutual, that is odd," his brother said. "Have you ever heard of this man or his insurance company? He gave the card to Verna. "No dear, never. There must be some kind of error. We should speak with him to make sure." Connor put the card in his vest pocket.

Sean got up suddenly from the table. "I have pressing business in town. Will you all be alright for an hour or two? Is there anything that needs doing?" Connor said, "Yes. The funeral director's check." He wrote a check and gave it to Sean to deliver. Sean left in a rush.

Clem Stanley was doing his own pencil-in-the-eye, boring police work in a town called Wilcox while his partner made ready to attend that sale. Wilcox was a picturesque, hilly place with a tannery that smelled like several tons of something had spoiled in the natural bowl of the river valley. He drove through Johnsonburg en route, which was not fragrant either. The paper mill gave off an acrid odor seven days a week. In Wilcox he shed his insurance man persona and began flashing his FBI badge and his large black-and-white of Gil Hammond and asking the standard questions. After having done this in two other very small settlements, he was glad to get a hit at last. The store clerk at the Anderson and Carlson store studied the picture only very briefly and said, "Oh yeah. Guy come in a couple of days ago and bought us out of bleach and petroleum jelly. Bought two five-gallon gas cans too. He said it was for his well supply outfit." Hammond was buying incendiary bomb building supplies.

"Could you swear to that? Look again at his picture and tell me. You're sure it's him. It's very important Mr.…"

"I'm Al Rhodes and I will be glad to testify if I'm still here. I'm going to boot camp in about a week."

"Don't worry about that. You keep your head down my friend, and good luck." Clem gave him a small notebook open to a blank page and asked for his name, address, and where he was to be stationed. "Have you seen him around since he was in here?"

"Yeah, a few times here and there. He's with another fellow and they are staying at a camp in Rasselas. They hang around at the McFarland House and drink and play cards. They'll probably have their dinner there tonight, I would guess."

Clem gave the store clerk a ten dollar bill, thanked him and headed directly to the McFarland House. It was noon. The sun streamed through the windows, their ancient glass distorted the view of a silver bridge trestle in a pipeline of green branches. He stood looking for a few minutes. It looked like a painting with impressionistic swirls of paint across the landscape. Out of the corner of his eye he saw a young guy with a neatly trimmed mustache and a checked shirt pulling bottles from a crate and stocking the bar shelves.

The head of a great, regal bull elk with the stillness of a satisfied sentry looked over the bar room of the McFarland House. The place was adorned with carved hardwood around the doors and windows. The long bar looked like it was a ton or more of solid cherry. A magnificent frame surrounded three giant mirrors showing some peeling on the back sides of their corners. The imperfection of aging of the mirrors only added to their appeal. If they could have recorded the years with hidden movie cameras behind them they would have shown soldiers celebrating a homecoming from the war between the states, Kane Rifle men or Bucktails maybe. Mostly such footage would reveal tired faces of defeated men with dullness in their pale eyes and red blotches on swollen skin, some with amputations, men who were stopping by at opening time to start their days. The solid old door swung open and two early patrons took bar stools close to the entrance in the thoughtless grace of habit. These two locals were too young to have seen civil war and too old for the present one. They were not his quarry.

The bartender said, "Good afternoon Helmer, Boltsie." He turned to Clem and said, "What can I get you?"

"Get theirs first." Clem moved down to the opposite end of the bar and took the last stool. He opened a copy of Outdoor Life. When the bartender had served drafts to Helmer and Boltsie, he finished stocking his last two booze bottles and returned. He smiled and pointed a finger. Clem said, "A bottle of lager. Whatever you like." When he returned with the beer, Clem showed him his badge concealed in the fold of the magazine. He whispered, "Agent Clement Stanley, sir." Clem paged ahead to where he had tucked his photograph of Gil Hammond. "Recognize him?"

"Yeah. Him and his friend are staying in a camp up in Rasselas. They've been here pretty much every day for a week or so. They are not the friendly kind. Is he wanted or something?"

"I'd rather not say but you know I'm not trying to locate them because they've won the sweepstakes." He gave the bartender a wad of bills. "Is there anything peculiar about these guys?"

"Just that they said they needed to find a store up in Sergeant or Kane that sells gallons of bleach. What do guys in a hunting camp need with gallons of bleach? I told them they could get it right here at Anderson and Carlson. He said they were all out of bleach over there. So I gave them two places in Kane to look and shrugged it off."

"I can double your tip if you can keep those guys here as long as possible tonight. I will be back with my partner as early in the evening as we can manage."

"No problem Mr. Stanley. Take your time. There's a five card stud game on tonight. They'll be here a good long time. It's a small-time game. The local car dealer, a couple of tannery guys and a Welshman who works for some drilling outfit. That's not going to mean trouble for us is it? The cops around here already know."

"I have a flexible memory about some things. So does my

141

partner when I ask him to. It's okay. Thanks." Clem placed an index finger across his lips. He quietly finished his beer, raised the empty green bottle to the two men at the other end of the bar and made his exit. He stopped by the Anderson and Carlson store. "Hello again Al. I need to borrow your telephone. It's private and it could take a while."

"Sure thing. Back in the office, first door on the left."

Clem called the Bogert and left a message for Osmund to call him at the general store when he came in for their lunch at one. He waited for his partner's return call while he sat chatting with Al to see if he knew anything in particular about the cabin his subjects were staying in, who owns the properties out there, and so on.

Years later, a reading of Osmund's duty report for the early part of the day read like a to-do list, minute details about nothing. The descriptions of events from noon onward were more like a dime novel.

That morning Agent Oliver Osmund could find no trace of Hammond or Sharp anywhere in Ridgway. One patron of a pool hall said that Sharp's keys were tethered with a Lincoln Log on a chain. Some of the hunting cabins around owned by a local real estate guy were done up that way. Osmund's early work that day had, according to his report, produced precious little. He mentioned Clem's message and subsequent conversation from the Anderson and Carlson store. The message said that Osmund should be ready to move on some things soon and that he, Clem, was returning to Ridgway shortly. He added as a by-the-way statement that the entire package would be gift-wrapped and waiting for them that evening in a Wilcox bar. After returning Clem's call, Osmund said he would be in the restaurant if Mr. Carthage should call again.

When Osmund turned to leave the desk there was a tall sandy-haired man dressed for labor right behind him. They collided and the man dropped a bag with nails in it. They hit the tile floor of the Bogert lobby like a metallic rainstorm. When Agent Osmund bent to help pick up the spilled nails, Sean could make out a service revolver in a holster under the man's suit coat. Osmund and the carpenter refilled the nail bag. "I'm very sorry," said the lying imposter. He was no insurance man.

"Are you an associate of Mister Carthage?" Sean inquired.

"Yes. We're partners. Can I help you?"

"My name is Sean Daugherty. Karl's uncle. I came by to let you and your company know of the unfortunate and untimely death of my nephew." Sean was barely able to get his announcement out before he began to sob. Agent Osmund said, "I'm so sorry." You look as if you should sit down." Sean's head was pounding, the effect of stifling a good cry. He was playing along with this cop or whoever he was. The lobby of the hotel took on the dizzying feel of a funhouse. The two men sat in a booth in the restaurant. Osmund ordered them two coffees. He said that if Sean was willing to wait, Mr. Carthage would be back at any moment. Sean said he needed to be with his family but he could spare five or ten minutes. When the coffee arrived Sean gave his cup no notice. There was a voice coming to him as though shouted from the street outside of the glass and oak front door some thirty feet away. He could make out most of what was being yelled at him, aware that it came from his own head. "Stop playing along. Get back to your brother and pay the grave diggers on your way." Sean slid out of his booth. And turned to go. Osmund slammed his coffee off-center onto its saucer. The heat shocked his fingers. He jumped between Sean and the restaurant doorway. Sean's demeanor shifted from mournful to menacing. "I have to go, mister." But Osmund didn't yield. Sean crossed his left leg next to Osmund's right leg, tripping and jerking him rudely back into the side of the booth he had just slid out of. There was a crashing of china and shriek of the booth scraping the floor. Osmund reached inside his jacket, not for his revolver but for his badge. Sean cocked back and swung hard connecting with the agent's eye. Customers drew back in a collective gasp. "Leave that gun right where it is, my friend. You can settle this with me later."

Osmund's instinct was to keep Sean at the restaurant but he made a quick judgment on his own. There were some events in the last few days that he found disturbing. Clem's methods appeared to be seriously flawed. It didn't make sense. They knew where Sean was every day and night and Clem had not yet gathered enough evidence to pick him up. The agents had made arrangements with the state police for Sean's detention at the local barracks where the two FBI men would interrogate Sean at length. Now, somehow their subject had unmasked them. Though he was mystified by his partner's reticence, his own judgment was to trust his mentor, and stay in step with Clem's handling of the Irishman. It made Osmund bristle to do it. There was also the matter of wanting with all that was in him to take Sean down in the pain and spitting anger of this insult. Osmund pushed all that aside.

He stood again and waved his arms to show he meant no retaliation. Sean said, "Listen," he said it in complete self-possession, his voice modulated down to a calmer level. "Give me an hour with my brother and his family. Come and get me at their place or wait until I get back here. You and your partner and myself, we have important things to talk about, and soon."

As Sean navigated the ruts in Whistletown Road, back in Wilcox, at the general store Clem and Al were interrupted a number of times by paying customers. Al introduced Clem as Will Carthage, as Clem had requested. The clerk said that the stranger was wasting his afternoon trying to sell him health insurance. "I'm about to be Uncle Sam's property for a while so Mister Carthage here is wanting me to buy a policy when I get back. By next Christmas, I hope."

Al didn't know who owned all of those hunting camps but he informed his new friend Clem as best he could. One cabin was being leased by some guys from Zelienople and another was owned by a couple of brothers from New York somewhere. Another was owned by a dairy man out there named Jake Braun. Different people leased Jake's place over the years. The places had names like The Seldom Seen or Lazy Eight Lodge. Al continued to traverse wildly from one topic to the other.

Al said that the McFarland House bartender's name was Cappy Smith and they were cousins. He had seen the Englishman (Yates) over at the McFarland House poker game and found out that, according to Cappy, he was not English at all, even though everyone in town had taken to calling him the Englishman. He was Welsh and he was a drilling outfitter. Clem asked him, "What was your impression of him?" Before Al gave him an answer he reached under the counter and retrieved a lunch sack. "Are you fond of licorice?" Clem said he was. "Red or black?"

"Black, but I'm not picky."

Al drew out a foot of black rope licorice and sliced it in two with a cheap Barlow knife exactly like the ones on a card next to the register. He evened up the ends so that the portions would be exactly equal. Clem took a bite of the rich, fresh confection just as the phone rang back in the office. He rushed to get it. "Clem, it's Oliver again. I've met our Sean Daugherty here at the hotel, right after I returned your call. Mix Wizard himself. He told me the Daugherty boy is dead and the family is back getting ready for the burial. He knows we are not here about his nephew's health insurance. After he made quite a scene here he took his leave to do some family business. I released him. Tell me that wasn't wrong." Oliver sounded more challenging than contrite.

"It's pretty much what I would have done at this point. Don't worry. We're going to put a ribbon on this one very soon."

18

BETTER THAN A LIE

Agent Osmund asked a frightened young waitress for a bar towel and a glass of ice. He wrote a note at the lobby desk with twenty sets of eyes on him. He went to his room. Howard Milton, the local game warden was hanging around the front desk enjoying a Cheroot. He waited for Osmund to ascend the stairs to his floor and asked the day clerk to give him the note Osmund had just left there. The clerk said, "Absolutely not."

"This is official Fish and Game business."

"Fish and Game my eye. Fishy, maybe. Can game wardens get search warrants?"

"Ah, come on Russ. Give it to me. I'll fold it back up and nobody will know."

"Go write some poaching tickets, Howie. You got no business here." He sat down, finished his cigar and struck up some conversations.

Agent Stanley arrived at the Bogert Hotel just as the game

warden was about to put his hat on and leave. When Milton saw the stranger rush into the restaurant and look around expectantly he froze in his tracks. The desk clerk stood with his arms crossed and glared at Milton. Clem spoke briefly to the waitress and walked with haste and purpose to the wooden counter in the lobby. He asked the day clerk if he had any messages. When Clem unfolded Osmund's note Milton drew close, craning his neck to read its contents. He said, "There may be evidence of a violation of state game laws there." Agent Stanley held the note out to him and as Milton reached for it the agent snatched it back behind his back to withdraw a wallet from his pants pocket. He presented his FBI shield to the game warden. Milton's uniform included a brass badge bearing his name. "Mister Milton. We have a jurisdictional problem I will now solve by telling you to get the hell away from me! If I see any unauthorized dead animals or trout, I assure you I will be in touch."

Upstairs in Osmund's room the two men looked at each other for several minutes as the loud plumbing swished and groaned from the hallway bath. Osmund closed his sore eye and applied his compress to it. "It's time you explained some of your methods to me in this investigation."

Clem was evasive. "Like I said before, you made the right choice, Ollie. You are a smart man with great instincts and you have taken a shot to your face on my account. Sorry for that. Get your coat and get back in character. We are going to see the Daughertys and interview Eunice face to face." Clem's *face to face* had a peculiar ring to it.

Agent Stanley was trying to tamp down his excitement over the Daugherty meeting. His elation had nothing whatever to do with how close they were to cracking a murder and a case of domestic spying. It was like a boiling cauldron under him. He had to allow the theory that he, Agent Clement Stanley, had been working under an unusual burden. He was covering it up. He was systematically destroying a fine professional resume over a girl who was probably too young for him. He was trying to spare the girl's uncle a possible deportation that would certainly bring the man's death in a matter of days. He was actively seeking leniency for an operative in a domestic terrorism plot. It was a move that called his soundness of mind into question. Clem saw Sean as a soldier but the man who signed the agent's paycheck would certainly see him as a spy. Agent Clem Stanley knew that this unfortified logic was less for the benefit of his soldier than for the soldier's niece, a girl who Clem had never laid eyes on. That particular shortfall would be corrected in a matter of a very few minutes.

On the short drive out along a set of well-kept lawns, shallow cliffs dug for the road bed and an occasional glimpse of lush green riverbanks, Osmund was prying anew at his partner's quiet defenses for a few answers. His niggling little questions were beginning to wear Clem down. "Please, Ollie. I'm thinking." Clem was thinking but he was not thinking very clearly. His nerves were raw and his ears were ringing. He had a feeling like you have when you dream that you are falling, hurtling into a chasm and there's no way to stop it. He let a tiny voice lie to him deep inside; *This is going to work out. Go on ahead as you planned.* But there was no substance to his plan, just drive and emotion. Plenty of emotion. For days he worked with his soul in bondage, thinking constantly about the girl. Now he was terrified like a schoolboy about meeting her. When he makes his play for her, what if she doesn't take to him? What if she turns out to be less than his dream of her? These were the thoughts tumbling in his mind all the way up that mountain. Not his strategy for dealing with Sean's family, not what he would say, what he would withhold or how he might play one Daugherty against the other. Oh, he was beaten before he started. This disaster was going to cost him his career. It would probably cost Osmund his too. Osmund with his pretty wife and two little sons. For a second, before he rounded a curve and spotted Connor Daugherty's front porch, he saw a flash of his terrible, reckless dive into this pit.

Clem was never as unprepared for an interview as he was for the ones to come. He drove on, even started to drive a little faster. Rocks flipped up and pounded the undercarriage. Osmund gave him a look like he had gone mad at the wheel so he backed off of the throttle. Finally they were knocking on the front door of the Daugherty's house.

Oliver kept quiet and followed Clem's lead. Clem introduced himself and Osmund as Mister Carthage and Mister Holstein, representatives of Rural Mutual Insurance. "Yes, come in," Connor said through a cloudbank of grief. Once inside, Clem took note of Sean's absence, at least from the kitchen and adjoining rooms. The crackerjack investigator had returned. The terrified sheep from the ride up the mountain was gone and the wolf began stalking again. He saw Verna sitting at the kitchen table with her tea cup. Eunice heard the front door close and came down the stairs.

Agent Stanley turned as her footfalls struck the floor behind him. "You must be Eunice."

She nodded and said, "Yes sir."

It was the strangest sensation Clem had ever known. He was transformed the moment she spoke. The terrified sheep was back. He felt the sweating, the weakness in his legs, a desert in his mouth. His body was telling him to sit down or fall. He even steadied himself with the back of Verna's kitchen chair. It was a bizarre disembodiment. His mind wavered like after a fist fight in a heat wave. The sight of her, her hair, her fair skin and her compact features, none of it had escaped him, it had, in fact, enraptured him more than he expected. The voice, so clear, unfiltered by a telephone line was a sublime string quartet in a velvety hall. But only for a moment.

Connor said, "These men are from an insurance company about a policy for your brother." He turned and asked Clem and Eunice to sit down. "Mister Carthage, I have to say, we are quite puzzled about your company and a policy we do not own."

"Don't worry Mister Daugherty, I will explain fully. We are not insurance claims reps at all. We are FBI and for the moment we are assisting local officials in a murder case."

Verna jerked her head forward into her hands as her elbows struck the table top, two distinct thuds merged into one louder one. Eunice looked at Connor and then at Clem. She forced her surprise to ratchet down into a slow clenched closing of her eyelids. For a long while there was only a ticking pendulum clock and a barely discernable wind.

"A murder?" Connor asked. "Who has been murdered?"

Clem looked at Verna through the web she made with her fingers and said, "I'm so sorry, Mrs. Daugherty." Then he looked over at Eunice. Her hair draping over one eye, her simple dress without pretention that was made for her. She wore no makeup nor did she need any. There was a beauty in her dark eyes that accompanied that face so well. A face nothing like he had imagined. Not prettier, not even close to his image of her from those phone calls. Her shoulders were straight and her arms, freckled and smooth. He wanted to touch them, to feel the alabaster.

Eunice looked Clem directly in the eye. In Philly she had imagined being with this grown man when they talked on the phone. It had been giddy and transient then. It was all guilt now -- indulging girlish fantasies, possibly at the moment of her brother's passing.

Clem told Connor that the murder victim was his father-in-law, that Sean was going to be taken for questioning as was his daughter. Connor said, "This is absurd. The local authorities deemed that incident an accident. And what could Eunice and my brother possibly have to do with any of it?"

"They are not suspected of any wrongdoing in this, Mister Daugherty. We just need to talk to them. Miss Daugherty will likely be detained for a matter of a few hours and returned here afterward. I will personally see to it that they are both treated well and made comfortable. This questioning is routine but necessary."

*   *   *

Three miles from his brother's home, Sean sat waiting at the funeral director's office. The secretary gave him some ice water which he drank down in one long swallow. When Sean's business was complete he hurried to his truck and drove down the alleys as fast as he could manage. He would go to Connor's place and wait for the detectives or federals or whoever they were to come and pick him up. He rehearsed to himself what he might say to the Daughertys about his predicament, about Yates's monstrous plan and his part in it. Would they understand that he was forced into this? Would Connor completely cave in from the two-edged grief of losing his son and now learning that his brother was involved in treachery and deceit? This was Connor's country and Sean had dishonored it even though the bomb was not armed, no fire started, and no American blood spilled in their town. Either way, Sean would take his lumps from Connor and from the authorities if it went that way. He was tired in a way he had never known before. Bone tired and soul tired. He was torn apart and beaten. He was done with all of it and ready for what was next. All he wanted now was for his family to keep him in their hearts. He would ask them to try and he would yield to a new, uncertain fate.

19

THE WRONG SIDE OF EVERYTHING

S ean tasted rusty steel and blood as he turned right onto
Whistletown road, the same washboard that Agents Stanley
and Osmund had traversed less than half an hour before. He
laughed bitterly about his plight. He had let that Clan na Casúr big
shot Tom Donleavy shove him into this hole. He took up the
cause, for that he had no shame or remorse. Connor was a strong
man, a thinking man. And Connor seemed to have no problem
with so many Irish being shoved into holes. Some were buried in
them. Maybe he was right to take a back seat, to sit by and accept
things as they were, too small and too insignificant to change any
of it. But Connor preached to his young charge about the political
process, slow as a snail and the instrument of the foreigners who
ran things in the North. After all that talk, Connor gave it all up
and went to Pennsylvania. It wasn't cowardice, it was smart. Sean
envied his brother. At least Connor was safe and his path was solid
and smooth. Nobody was hunting him. He had a fine position
and good wages, land of his own, and friends. Sean had a single
truth as his healing balm; he knew he had done everything he could
to protect Connor's life.

They would be putting Karl in the ground in a few days. Sean envied him a little too. Maybe Sean could bury his past with him even if he was not permitted to attend the burial service. He could be rid of people like Yates forever. He wanted to make something out of the scrap of his old life, to change things somehow. He wanted to run to something because running from everything had not served him very well. His old ways, being on the wrong side of everything had done nothing but leave him tired.

None of these things seemed to carry much weight after his brother's house came into view. There was a pall on the place that he could feel and see. There, under the maple next to the porch was the government men's sedan. He parked and walked mechanically into the house.

As Sean passed through the doorway, Osmund put his hand on the handle of his revolver. Clem had his back to the door and was answering Verna's questions with very little detail, apologizing for his obfuscation, unable as he was to discuss evidence or other specifics about the case. How he had wished for a meeting with Verna's fair daughter without the fetid cloud of family trouble his presence in their home had amplified! "I can only state, Mrs. Daugherty, that we know enough to gather more evidence here in town and, with luck, help bring your father's killer to justice." As he said those words, Osmund said, "Excuse me, Agent Stanley… Sean Daugherty…"

"Well, Mister Sean Daugherty, I trust you will forgive my deception at our first meeting down there in Bennet's Valley. I am not an insurance man. I'm Special Agent Clement Stanley, FBI." Clem stepped forward, hand extended, which Sean shook with a blank expression. Clem said, "I was just speaking with your brother's wife about a case we will need your help with. It concerns some suspects in the murder of a Karl Lundquist and you and your niece may be very helpful in our investigation. We have a room at the local Pennsylvania State Police barracks where we can talk in confidence and relative comfort. Would you and Miss Daugherty accompany us this afternoon?" Clem turned to Eunice and felt his heart soften into fresh clay just looking her in the eye. She nodded and even smiled. "We can drive you out there."

"Of course." Sean was torn. He wanted to get things out in the open with Connor right away. It had been delayed first for the Philadelphia trip and now he was forced to delay it yet again. It would be a disgrace heaped on him if Connor learned of Sean's crimes from the newspaper or the local police. He was sure that the State Police would simply keep him. Everything was wrong, the wrong time, the wrong people and place, the wrong country, and he was as he had been all his life, unable to become a real part of anything. Still, he played along with the FBI man and let the events unfold out ahead of him like the dark, familiar dead-end road directly out of one of his dreams.

Osmund opened his rear car door and motioned for Sean and Eunice to get in. Clem pointed to his own chest and then toward the rear seat. As Osmund got his car in gear, Clem told him, "Sorry to treat you like our chauffer, Ollie. I've got a bad neck and I want to talk to the girl and her uncle." There was nothing wrong with Clem's neck but he rubbed it a little. This seating arrangement got him closer to Eunice and gave him a good look at both of their faces. He was starting the interview process right away. Clem said, "Thank you both for coming along." Then he waited to see if anyone would break the silence.

Eunice looked out through the window on her side. Sean stared at the back of Osmund's head. The air in the car was alive with electric sparks snapping between the Irish man and his niece. Nobody said anything the entire way down the mountain. When they reached the bottom, Clem asked Oliver to turn left. "But the barracks is…"

"I know where it is, Ollie, but we need to take a side trip." They drove to the Bogert Hotel. In the lobby, Clem handed Sean the key to his room and said, "Take Miss Daugherty to the room and have a talk. Get things settled with your family. When you are ready we will head to the police barracks and the questioning."

The two went up to the third floor. When they had closed the door to Clem's room it was a clear signal that echoed in the stairwell and off of the small ceramic tiles in the lobby. Osmund was angry and frustrated. "What in the name of God are you doing?" He struggled to keep his voice down. Do you want them to get their stories together? How do you know the girl isn't involved?"

"She's not."

"How can you be sure? You keep getting more and more haywire as this investigation goes along. What rules are there left to break?"

"Take it easy, Ollie. I know what I'm doing."

"That's nonsense. You have flipped over a girl. A girl! You are squandering your life and possibly mine on a young girl still wet behind her ears. I have reached my limit. I'm calling the AIC in Philly. Holy jumpin' shit, Stanley."

Clem stood still. He looked stunned. Osmund was really over some edge or other. The AIC Osmund mentioned was the Agent in Charge of the Philadelphia office. Morris Springs. Clem had never heard that kind of language out of Osmund before. Never as much as a single hell or damn. He wouldn't use the word whore, even when it fit. It was just too strong for him, a word that, as Agent Stanley pointed out to his partner, was in the King James Bible. Osmund used a euphemism: lady of the evening.

"Okay Agent Osmund, call Springs if you must, but I would wait and see what happens, just till later tonight." Clem was stalling. He knew that Special Agent Springs would be attending his daughter's piano recital that evening in Upper Darby and after that, a reception for a retiring bureau chief. "Just wait, could you?"

"I can't."

"At least wait until we drop Sean off, have a quick round of questions and then we'll go pick those bums up at the McFarland house. Don't you want to collar them first, get them out of circulation? I'm begging you, Ollie. Springs will call in the OSS. By the time they get here our three little saboteurs will be done with their game and disappear. Do you really want Springs to get his hands in this now? Springs will give you his own set of orders. He'll expect you to assist the OSS guys with the arrests in Wilcox and then he'll have me turn in my badge to you."

Osmund was calming down. Clem could see that his partner was giving his haywire proposal some thought.

"Is that what you want, Ollie, to be in charge? Is that your desire?"

Osmund had now arrived at a slow simmer. He wouldn't look at Clem for a long time. Clem was trying to read his partner's face. The result of this standoff was a strange dance in the hotel lobby, with the two men twirling around each other in the middle of the floor. Osmund pushed both hands deep into the pockets of his jacket, then removed them and adjusted his shirt cuffs. "That is not my desire. My desire is to save my own backside before you sink this investigation like a leaky rowboat. I can't take your place, not yet. I've never seen a better cop than you. But lately..."

"Lately I have been a slight bit off-center, uh, more than usual. But right now, as I said, I know exactly what needs to be done. That girl and her uncle need to have a very private word up there in that room. You have to trust me this one last time. This is going to make all the difference. This moment right here." Clem had both of Osmund's forearms gently in his hands, messing up the agent's meticulous alignment of his cuffs. Osmund looked at his cuffs as if to say, "Hey! Darn it, I had those just right." Osmund backed up a step or two. He finally looked at Clem's face. "I must be insane. Tell me I'm not insane. Of course I want that collar. I will wait but you better have something really big to show me. This better be good or so help me, I'll..."

"You'll cuss at me again. That was a good one, "Holy jumpin' shit. That your first time on the profane train, Ollie?"

Osmund laughed. Clem was right. Every powerful man on either side of the law was adept at swearing. The two of them had covered Osmund's abysmal use of profanity while in character many times before. His laughter was born out of those memories but also out of his sense of inadequacy. That feeling of weakness, the worldly obstruction Osmund was facing brought a sobering hush. He quickly stopped. Without a hint of a smile, he said, "This better be a doozy. You'll be the death of me yet, Special Agent Clement Stanley."

The two agents sat in hard steel and wood chairs near the front desk. The desk clerk asked if he could be of service and, "How's your business going in town, gentlemen?" The clerk figured out that these men were not who they said they were just after the incident in the restaurant earlier. He stared at the sore-looking eye that Osmund was sporting and winked at him. The way he asked his question was as transparent as his other tells, the casual backward tilt of his head, his obvious effort to portray nonchalance; these were signals from a man who believes that something is up. This was certainly not Philadelphia where you could blend in and nearly disappear, where your movements are anonymous. Here you might as well give Chief Editor Gibbs a daily schedule of your workday. Your business is the obsession of a dozen whispering mouths anyway. The agents let the high eyebrows go by. In a few hours they would raid the McFarland House poker game and lock a trio of dangerous men in a jail cell. Just another workday. Osmund said to the clerk, "We may be here just a day or two more."

The clerk faded back into his doorway which led to the hotel bar, nodding and smiling as he peddled back. Footfalls, two sets of them, echoed in the lobby. It was Eunice and Sean.

Eunice made a blowing sound and looked downward. Sean looked first at her then at the two FBI men. He looked back at her again and nudged at her chin. She smiled through tightened lips and breathed deeply. Sean said, "I believe we have business elsewhere, gentlemen. Is it necessary for the girl to go along?"

Clem said, "We can discuss things with her later, if it suits."

Osmund looked on quietly. He began to think he might try some whiskey again before this evening was through. He was reaching a point at which his nerves had become so raw that virtue was beginning to lose its luster. Sean stepped forward and looked Osmund in the eye as he addressed Clem. "Agent Stanley, I am indebted to you for what you have done for Eunie here, and for me. She put me straight about everything." While her uncle was addressing the FBI men, Eunice was looking into Clem's eyes. She had wanted so badly to despise him. For her, Clement Stanley was, at first her enemy, the enemy she had handed her uncle over to willingly. Clem was the scapegoat for her guilt and pain. She confessed the guilt only moments before to Sean upstairs in Clem's room. Things had changed dramatically for her but in a way she had not expected. The change was like watching the Clarion flow freely one winter's night, then returning to find it frozen over the next morning. Now that Sean had absolved her she had no need to resent Clem. She was beginning to look differently at the man she had held in such contempt. Even Osmund, who had been so awkward, now seemed to her a pillar of a man.

Sean draped his arm over Eunice's shoulder, "You did right. You and your brother, may God bless him with rest." Osmund believed that Sean Daugherty was the most perceptive and courageous man he had ever met. He described these feelings in his written report.

Eunice was privately having her epiphany while Osmund was having his. He was also feeling proud of Clem now, and proud that he had participated in this brilliant piece of gamesmanship. *Gamesmanship* was the word in his head, echoing within something more hollow than it should have. He discarded it, exchanging it for some softer words, a phrase: expert reading of people and their hearts.

Sean sensed a dramatic turnabout he was convinced was happening in Osmund, he could see it in his body language, hunching as he did on the check-in desk. Osmund straightened bolt stiff at the wonderment. This amazing girl and her dead brother had something that their uncle would prize and detest all at once. It became clear for Agent Osmund when Sean smiled at him. No, they would not need the girl for questioning. She had done her job and served her purpose. It must have been the hardest thing she had ever done. You don't betray your blood.

But you have to set things right. This girl is a rock! Osmund wished that he could have met the brother she lost.

Osmund was assigned to Eunice's ride home. She started talking the moment he wheeled his sedan out of the Bogert parking lot. "I ratted my own dear uncle out. Is that the right way to say it? I turned him in, I betrayed him."

"It's not that cut-and-dried, Miss Daugherty. It's just not. Did you speak to him at all about your grandfather's murder? Did your conversation go into any of that history? Your brother knew something was very wrong with all of that, didn't he?"

"Karl was onto Uncle Sean. He knew about the plans for the fire bomb. He was pretty sure that this guy from Ridgway, Mickey Mahoney killed my grandfather. I figured you guys would get around to the bombing plan. But I'm glad you let me talk to my uncle. Is he going to jail?"

"I would have to say, yes. Maybe he'll be relatively young when he gets out. It's hard to tell at this point."

Eunice looked out her car window at the last two houses in town going North. "Mister Osmund, my uncle said something that really scared me. You have to keep a close watch on him. He said he has to kill a man, Merle Yates. You won't let him do that? Tell me you won't."

Osmund swallowed hard. He found a wide spot on the shoulder of the street which some folks with a house two hundred feet up a steep green bank had carved out. He turned to Eunice unsure of what he might say. He resisted his urge to violate a principle that he once lived by: never get personal with an informant. This left him muttering and holding a hand over his mouth. She had a peculiar look on her face. Osmund understood his partner's fall at once, and he saw clearly in an almost frightening flash, the youth and innocence being washed over in her, leaving a penetrating gaze full of the stuff of pain and crisis, and yet it was a look full of resolute strength. Where had she come by it? How could her eyes give so much away and hold so much in reserve at the same time? Then she said softly. "Did you want to tell me something, Agent Osmund?" He took the hand from his lips The words flowed uninhibited. "Merle Yates is the worst kind of rat and I wouldn't mind taking a shot at him myself."

Eunice looked very briefly at Osmund again, this time she smiled tightly, in her guarded and measured way. There was no approval and no condemnation in her glance, just a weariness, just, *I see*. Then she grasped Osmund's arm above his elbow and made the slightest caress. He looked down at that hand and, in her silence imagined what the words that went with the gesture would be; Do what you must do, Agent Osmund, but don't you think there has been enough killing? That silence, fertile with imagination, continued to the Daugherty's front doorstep. "You and your partner... please be careful," she said.

Osmund headed back down the mountainside. Eunice waited on her porch to see if she could put all of her thoughts into some kind of order. Her uncle did not hold her decision against her. In the agent's hotel room she recounted to Sean her reluctance to give the FBI too much information about him, but when she changed her mind on the phone with Clem and Osmund she was deceiving herself. She knew that the investigation into their grandfather's murder would lead them to all of the men whose names were hidden in Sean's bed-frame locker. Back there in Clem's room Sean had taken both of her hands in his own and said, "Yours was exactly the right choice. It's what I would have done if I were in your place." She leaned back against a pillar on the porch. She had a feeling of weightlessness, near giddiness and in the midst of it came another thought: what am I to do with Special Agent Clement Stanley? This one she put on the shelf. It would be best to wait until the storm in her heart calmed down. She would not be too forward, especially under these circumstances. It wasn't proper for a young lady to pursue a man too aggressively. She would wait but if he made no move in say, two weeks she would have to make one of her own. She still had his phone number. For now it would be best to see if her folks needed anything, make some hot cocoa and later read herself to sleep.

Early that evening Osmund drove the State Police barracks. In a small room full of bookcases and a few clusters of framed photographs of revered troopers there was a table and three chairs. Sean sat in handcuffs leaning forward and looking down at the tabletop. He was sweating. Clem sat across from him taking some notes. He motioned to Osmund to take the remaining chair. Minutes later, Clem said, "Sean, I need for you to tell us what you know. We have somewhere to be and we are about to get very busy with this case. I think agent Osmund has some information he gleaned from an interview with Mickey Mahoney. It may help you decide how much you would like to disclose. Oliver."

Osmund said, "Mister Mahoney, I understand, had an altercation with your nephew on Thanksgiving Day." Sean nodded. "Is it true," asked Clem, "that you had a fight on a state park job site with Mister Mahoney yourself?" Sean spoke for the first time in fifteen minutes. "If you mean Mickey Mahoney, that would be right. The man has no character. He is a waste of good air. He needed some wisdom and guidance about whose young niece he should be drooling over. He was most definitely out of line. Now he's in prison where he belongs."

Osmund took a small notebook from his pocket. He glanced at it regularly as he recounted Mickey's statement about Merle Yates's culpability in the Karl Lundquist case. He said that Eunice was not aware that Mickey had not participated in the beating but had driven Yates to and from the scene. Sean straightened up. He asked for water. Osmund went for a cup of water from a fountain near the door. Clem said, "Yates is ready to fire-bomb the Elliot plant. Our friends at OSS discovered that Yates made a change in personnel, a Canadian Mix Wizard, and we've learned that a new diesel-electric sub engine is being tested in a matter of days, on the night shift. Yates wants the bombing to proceed on that same shift as he originally planned it. Your brother is scheduled to work at Elliot that evening."

"That was not the agreement I made."

"Yates is not the agreement kind, Sean. Somewhere along the way he decided you weren't up to his expectations. I've studied this guy and dozens more like him. He was going to be rid of you and your brother, the brains behind the engine. You, mister Daugherty are a realist. Therefore, you were well aware that it's a death sentence to inform on a man like Merle Yates. He knew you might not have the stomach for this particular project. The interesting thing is that he has kept you out of his story. Nobody knows that he wanted you dead, not even Donleavey. You were a target even before you backed out. Yates is a realist too. You would have been honor-bound to avenge your brother's death. But it's good that none of Yates's higher-ups know about you. When Yates and his pair of goons are caught, you get out of this without a stain. Except, of course for your problems with the law."

"Why tell *me* this? How do I know you aren't making this up?"

"Because Yates is one of a half dozen people we have some interest in, people here in the US, in Ireland, and places like Nova Scotia and Quebec." People we would very much like to talk to from Clan na Gael and some other organizations. Some we want out of circulation. People with access to guns and explosives. I have a list of names I'm happy to show you. Many are folks you are familiar with. You've got to get wise, Sean. OSS doesn't know who the original Mix Wizard was. That was my doing. I kept your name clean. You may be able to assist our efforts to put some of these criminals away. If you like living here, hell, if you just like living, you are going to have to put up or shut up."

"How can I help you from a federal prison somewhere here in the states?" Sean looked at the list that Clem gave him. "Sure, I've heard some of these names, and I have even met some of them. Where would you like me to start?"

Osmund said, "Begin with Yates and his friends, Hammond and Sharp."

Sean sat back in his chair, holding the list in his shackled hands. "If your raid goes wrong, you can find these guys and probably all the bomb materials at the Lazy Eight Lodge. The road to it is the closest one to the Braun Dairy on the right side of the paved road. Keep a watchful eye on Sharp. He's the goon among them. You know from that coded list that he's Violent Acts. He is that for a reason. He's insane. You can't anticipate what he'll do. I've never known a man who is more of a brute. Maybe if you surprise him you can take him. Even Hammond would tell you the same. Sharp always has a boot knife taped under his sock. Yates will likely try to run and you'll have to disarm him. He has a fondness for the pistol, he does. I had an idea he was going to be shut of me soon. He thought I was weak, that I lost my head back home over a girl. That's a notion he got from Donleavey, the man who paid my way. But then, you know all about him." As Sean said this, Osmund pulled his fedora over one eye and looked across the table at Agent Stanley. He gave his partner a tiny chuckle, a derisive snorting laugh and added, "Skirt chasing. That's a pattern we sometimes see."

"Well they read me wrong. I should have stayed in Armaugh. I knew I had to pay the piper soon enough but I was always looking for a way out. I was sick of the bombs and the piddling little attacks back home. Now they wanted to make trouble here. I lived and worked in these mountains and I was happy with that. I couldn't go through with it. It sickened my heart. Please tell my brother and his wife and daughter, I was never going to arm that bomb."

"Maybe we can fix it where you can tell them yourself someday Sean." Clem circled the table until he had gone around it one full turn. He bent close to Sean's ear and leaned one-handed on his shoulder. "I thought you may be more willing to help, now that you know that Yates is responsible for the death of Karl Lundquist. I read you wrong a bit myself. You were ripe enough to turn before I met you. That makes you what we call an asset." He freed Sean's shackled wrists. Sean said to Osmund, "Mister Osmund, forgive my earlier outburst at the hotel." The two shook hands. Osmund said, "Consider that forgotten," disregarding some dull aching. "That was a good punch you landed. I never saw it coming. Aw, let's just go bust up a poker game." They took separate cars, needing to reserve the backseats for some soon-to-be handcuffed spies. Osmund rode alone.

20

THE MCFARLAND HOUSE GAME

The two plain Plymouth sedans cruised along the patched asphalt in the early evening. A small flock of starlings passed over them, darting and weaving against the cloudbank. Sean watched them find maple branches to rest on. He cranked his window down to hear their invisible squawking in the canopy. He longed to be invisible himself. He wanted to erase his past and some of the more dishonorable things he had been part of. No, he never bombed anyone. He was an apprentice who had grown weary of the warring tribes, sickened by the first bombed-out house he saw smoldering in the mist. The smoky odor of flesh and the flock of vultures drifting to the random places their mindless nature dictated to them. It was a clumsy bird ballet. Mindless. The killing and the shooting, the throwing of rocks, accomplished nothing. His brothers in arms were so sure it would change things. The only change was the depth of the commitment of their enemies. There was no winning or losing; there was instead death and imprisonment. It kept him awake at night like a constant hum. He wondered if accepting Clem Stanley's offer would muffle or extinguish that hum and give him some peace. He hoped he could have that peace one day here in America. Underneath his hope was a foolishness, the thin wisp of euphoric liberty for a few precious moments in which the noise of his fear was gone and the exuberance of a flock of starlings took its place, resting in a tree with no evil portent, unlike the superstition of a murder of crows. He shrugged off these thoughts and spoke to his new mentor.

"Do you like motorcycles, Agent Stanley?"

"I like to watch them race. They have climbing races on a hillside near Philly on Sundays. It's thrilling and unpredictable. You know somebody is going down off those two wheels. It's not a matter of if, but when. I guess that's why I go. Free beer is another reason."

"Have you ridden one, ever?"

"Once. And I went down. I hardly got it moving and down she went. Took a patch of skin off my knee and my elbow. Naw, I watch some other fools try to keep them up while I drink beer and try to pick a winner. They make some fine German beers in Philadelphia."

"My friend Gorski has an Indian. It's fast and wild. He lets me take it around these fire lines and wood roads. Sometimes on the paved ones too. I've taken my girl out on it. She really likes riding on the back of it. She cries out, "whee" like a school girl. I think it makes her horny."

"I've heard about that. There's a woman who races on Sundays. I think it just makes her mean."

"You know, Clement, once I take this new road, this opportunity you are trying to give me…"

"You understand, there are no guarantees, right?"

"I do. I'm just exchanging one peril for another. It seems as though I'm doomed to a life of looking over my shoulder."

Clem took his eyes off the road for a kindly smile. "Well, my friend, you makes your choices and you lives with them. But don't think of it that way. Think of the good work you'll be doing. Not to sound corny but you can save some lives. You will be paid well and we'll look after you. Keep your nose clean and who knows, you could be badged. You'll have the full force of the Bureau behind you."

"A cake walk then?"

"Shit, no. I've been killed in my sleep a hundred times. Ollie sleeps like a baby but he's kind of jumpy sometimes. He gets stuck on things that don't matter. I think the guy takes all his fears and smothers them in his rules and regs. He's a fucking cub scout sometimes. He's a good partner and a very smart man. Like you, Sean. You just have to wise up, like I've been telling you. You know, it is entirely possible that Donleavy gambled on your own survival here in America. Think about it. If you proved yourself with Yates all the better, if you didn't, Donleavy was probably content to let Yates carry out your sentence."

Sean studied the side of Clem's face and searched through his memory for a single reason that the agent could be wrong. When he could find nothing in those stores, he felt the embarrassment of this near-fatal shortfall of wisdom. He felt fear come on him like a frost. He questioned the odds of his own survival in his new life. There was some scant comfort that the old cliché, live and learn had taken on a whole new caste. He thought about other things, like his debt to Agent Clement Stanley.

Clem straightened his spine against the back of his seat. "You have some very smart people on your side. Eunice Daugherty for example. If we don't get killed making these arrests, I'm going to marry her."

From his position behind the lead car, Osmund saw Sean jab his head back in a great laugh and wondered what he could possibly have to laugh like that about. He drove on with his grip tighter on the wheel than he needed, following behind his partner as they slowed down coming into the village. They passed a high bank to their right with lush green around the rocks and on the left, the bend in the river which he could see through a gap in the trees. He was admiring the wildness of the river bank for just a second. He relaxed his grip on the wheel and grasped tightly again, until his knuckles ached. He was taking deep breaths. Sean turned around and looked through the rear window at Osmund as though the too-tight agent were in the back of Clem's car and Sean was simply checking whether he had understood the joke. Osmund muttered to himself, "Eyes straight ahead Mister Daugherty, and you better hope things don't go sideways on us. I wish I could be so jolly at times like this."

They parked behind the McFarland House where there were some wooden steps with a hand rail of two-by-fours and a door. Clem took a revolver from his glove box where it lay sheathed in a leather shoulder holster. He loaded it, spun the cylinder, clicked the safety on and handed it to Sean. "You stand by the rear fender of this car. If one of those bastards runs out this door, shoot him immediately and don't patty-cake about it. Have you ever fired a gun at a man before?"

"I've been where the bullets were flying, but no. Deer and squirrels don't shoot back."

"I'll grant you that. You'll be fine."

Sean stood there with his back to the Clarion, the River of Pain. He had heard the stories from Gorski about the Indians, the places they camped and the places where they must have forded. They gave it that name. He told Sean about their wars with other tribes. From his post, he could hear the racket of birds settling in behind him. Many had flown over his head to their roosting places, the river's great maples, elms and chestnuts. He daydreamed about the Clan na Gael's Thompsons nested as they were in straw in the crates, shiny and black, menacing. He held one across his chest while Stephen Hayes laughed at him. Stephen laughed at everyone like God had put humans on earth for his entertainment. He laughed when he was nervous. The boys were told to leave the crates alone but Stephen had to open it. The gun had been heavier than Sean imagined and he grunted a little when he hoisted it up. He remembered that day now and envisioned having it back across his chest, much the superior weapon to the .38 in his sweating hand. He thought back to the night Stephen was shot and how the boy laughed at the men who killed him. Sean certainly had traded one peril for another. Perhaps tonight he would learn which was worse.

There was a gunshot, some yelling he couldn't make out and another shot. Somebody yelled, "Boltsie! My God Boltsie's been shot!"

Inside, the barroom was alive with immediate chaos. Boltsie was already dead from a shot that went through the back of his neck. Men were lying on the floor with their hands holding their pates. Sean heard the ruckus of a table being overturned from where he stood, that strangely didn't crash on the tavern's floorboards. There was breaking glass and running. Sean started forward but stopped himself and maintained his post.

Osmund was on the floor moaning and gasping for breath, the table on his chest. Yates's first shot, aimed at Osmund from under the table top missed the agent and shattered a Cognac bottle in Cappy Smith's hand. He was still holding the neck of the bottle with its fancy wooden cap. That second shot missed its mark because Clem had hurled a bentwood chair and struck Yates's shoulder just as he pulled the trigger. Sean finally decided to move at about the same moment Yates did. Yates was at the door and Clem had drawn a bead on his head when he heard the thud of Sean's approach to the door.

A moment later Sean jumped, vaulting the two wooden steps to the landing outside of the door. With his free hand he steadied himself on the two-by-four railing and it shoved two nasty splinters into his palm. He stopped to lick the blood and the door burst open with a loud smack against the outside wall. The birds panicked and rose as one giant flock, creating a sudden, thunderous mass of wing beats. Yates, pearl handled Colt in hand, smashed into Sean with such force the two men broke through the rail and onto a cinder patch. Sean's gun was nowhere to be found. He looked Yates in the eyes. Yates sprayed spit into Sean's face. Sean smelled the cognac his attacker was panting through. Enraged and shocked, Yates said, "You? You little Irish pissant, you." Yates was straddling him now as he lay on his back. He began to pound Sean's jaw with his left hand as his right index finger found the inside of his trigger guard. He jerked the trigger but the gun remained silent. He had bumped the safety on during his collision with Sean. Sean instinctively punched across his chest into Yates's wrist. He swung across and down hard against Yates's gun hand and the pistol flipped into Sean's left armpit. He caught the muzzle in his right hand and swung a hard backhand, placing a perfect blow with the gun's pearly handle on Yates's left temple. Yates pressed his head as blood ran through his fingers. He grunted and swayed like a drunk in a saddle.

Sean shoved at Yates's chest and he fell between his feet. He switched off the safety with a familiar motion, having done it a thousand times with his own Colt. He stood over Yates. "Goodbye Merle," he said, but he pushed the safety back on and tossed the pistol across the road into some milkweed. He turned Yates over, pulled his wrists behind him and held them there. His hand burned where the splinters sent shockwaves to his brain.

When Clem came out shoving Hammond and Sharp ahead of him, Osmund kept a gun on the thugs and said, "Hold up a minute." Clem stopped and said whoa to his two captured beasts. Osmund tossed Sean a pair of hand cuffs. The agent was dazed, hunched, limping. Sean clamped Yates's wrists. Yates was placed into the back of Osmund's car. Osmund got ropes from his trunk and hog tied the Welshman. Clem deposited the other two in his car, similarly roped and cuffed. Sean stopped the swing of the car door with that splintered hand and bled generously on the window glass. "One second," he said. He removed Sharp's boot knife from his roped ankle, making certain that the medical tape that held it there harvested a small bale of his leg hairs in the bargain.

Sean began to work on the slivers with the tip of Sharp's knife, pausing from his self-surgery to open the front door of the Plymouth. Clem said, "Uh-uh, you're not going." He drew him away from the car and spoke in hushed tones. "I need you to go down the block to a blue house with a white fence behind the Anderson and Carlson general store. Go in the back door and wait for Cappy. He and the cops from the poker game will be cleaning up and taking care of poor old Boltsie's body. Ollie, give us your hat, would you?"

"It's a Montecristi, Clem."

"Sean will replace it. Won't you Sean?"

"I never have been much for the hats, Clem."

Clem crowned Sean with the fine fedora. "Keep the brim over your eyes. Don't want anyone to see you."

Sean obliged by brimming his eyebrows, putting his face in a pool of darkness. Osmund winced as Sean left a small smear of blood on the brim. "Why my hat?" Osmund whined.

"It's the only hat we got and it fits him too. Looks very smart."

"Yeah, why the hat?" Sean asked just before he freed some of the wood from his hand.

"Because you were killed in this unfortunate incident tonight, Sean. Dead men don't go walking the streets of Wilcox now do they?"

Osmund gave the last whisper of their huddle behind the McFarland House. "Oh, fantastic. A dead guy owes me for a hat."

Sean walked along the alley to the blue house. There was a bottle of Kentucky Bourbon on the kitchen table. He switched on the radio and listened to some soothing symphonic music and finished the surgery on his hand. His head pounded and his back ached and bled into the waistband of his shorts. Sean had two drinks and fell asleep in his chair, his head on his arms.

As Sean slumped over Cappy's table and snored, the two Agents were just entering the lobby of the Bogert Hotel. Their suspects were booked and safely caged up. Clem paused at the front door and Osmund put his foot on the first stair when he realized that his partner was not with him. He turned around. Clem stood at the door with one hand on the doorjamb as if he felt week or dizzy. "Plans for the rest of this evening?" asked Osmund.

"I have got to talk to the girl, to Eunice, to Miss Daugherty."

"Case-related, of course." Osmund turned to go to his room. "But tell me immediately when you get back. I will be drafting our report."

"Uh, maybe you shouldn't wait up for me."

"Why not. Oh, Clem, no. The timing is all wrong for that."

"Damn the timing. I'm not having this conversation on the telephone."

"I would say it's your funeral but it is her brother's, Clem. And never mind all the rest of what she's been through. Use your head, will you? Take it easy. You can come back to town after things cool down for her."

"Yeah, that was what I thought. But no, Ollie. This cannot wait." He hurried to his car and was gone in an instant.

When he knocked at the Daugherty's door at ten p. m. Eunice answered. "Hello Eunice. May I see you for a few minutes?"

"Certainly. Is there something wrong? Is my uncle alright?"

"Yes. Everything is alright concerning this case. Well your uncle is and is not doing very well." Eunice was puzzled by his remark and her face telegraphed that message to her visitor. "Come in. If you want to talk to mom and dad, we'll have to wake them."

"No, it's you I came to see."

The two sat and drank hot cocoa until two in the morning. At first, Eunice told Clem that her heart and her soul were like whirling tornadoes. He said his were too. After a time her reticence began to dissolve. If it was reckless or forward, she no longer cared. Clem said, "Look at me Eunie, tell me what you see." Something broke away from her like an ice jam racing away on the current. She laughed and then went silent to form her answer just right. "You live in a shell where you think and you calculate. You take things apart and you break them down to the very basic and the simple. You really know people. Being the big, tough and proper FBI man that you are, it must have been hard for you to come here tonight." Opening up to him was so easy. She listened to a call from deep inside and told him her real feelings, which they agreed had come on them both too suddenly. There were facts and there was evidence. There were truths and there were absolutes. There were, most importantly these feelings that they shared. Gone was her desire to protect her feminine reputation, as she had been taught. Nothing she had been taught could prepare her for any of this. Her honesty rushed into him with such force that it unlocked the vault where he kept his true feelings. He had nothing to lose by telling her exactly how he had felt the moment he saw her that same afternoon in her parents' house. They were swept up in all of it. A thousand philosophers and a ship load of poets would never have words for any of it. Still they found their own words and before he returned to the hotel, the two of them had pledged their love for one another. It was the craziest and most sensible thing either of them had ever done.

*   *   *

Two hours later, back in Wilcox, Cappy shook Sean awake. Sean had a cloth napkin tied around his hand and his headache was gone. He picked his head up from the tabletop. Cappy asked, "Sean, is it?"

"It is. Are you Cappy?"

"Yeah. I gave everybody one more round, cleaned up and closed the bar early. One of the regulars got shot and killed and I had a close one myself. Your bedroom door is straight ahead at the top of the stairs, got its own bathroom. That FBI man says to get some rest. You're going to Philadelphia tomorrow."

At 6 a. m. Sean lay dreaming fitfully and nearly awake. There was a hammer tied with a rope trailing his ankle as he descended Cappy's stairs. His suitcase was open and clothes fell out leaving a trail of his laundry behind him on the stairs. He had a nickel in his hand for the phone booth in Cappy's kitchen. He was going to call Cleo and say goodbye. A Russian ballet blared from the radio. A soft movement began as he thumped his way down. Soon the bumping of the hammer stopped and a muted voice called to him, "Sean, you have company downstairs."

Sean splashed cold water on his face and tarried at the mirror for a minute. The Irishman who looked into the mirror, with his swollen eye and whiskers was somber. The American man looking back at him was feeling cocksure and proud. They both smiled but for different reasons. The Irishman had to die to accomplish anything worthwhile. His was the sardonic smile of finality that says, the joke is on me. The American was smiling because he was given a rare chance to show what he was made of and he would get to do it with the slate clean. Every mistake and misstep, every deed that brought shame was the deed of a dead man. He went downstairs.

As he passed through Cappy's narrow hall to the kitchen he heard his host say, "I've got errands to run." Cappy turned to his visitors. "You government men, uh, and lady probably have secret things to talk about anyways." And the door closed.

Osmund stood at a window and parted the curtain to be sure no one was listening in or lingering about. Clem poured milk into Eunice's coffee.

"Eunie. You're drinking the coffee now, are you?"

"Good morning Sean. Yeah, I found out I like it with milk, no sugar."

Sean realized that Agent Stanley was not joking about his

intentions to wed his niece. He was trying to settle into agreement about that until he saw what a pretty young lady she had become, a woman who makes decisions of her own and doesn't look back. Clem gave Sean a hug across his shoulders like he could read what he had been thinking. "Your niece came by to say goodbye, Sean. Unfortunately everyone else, and I mean everyone else, is going to believe you were shot in the face and you'll get a grave on a nice, green hill in Ridgway. What a wake, eh Ollie." Osmund said, "Good riddance to a real scoundrel, pass me the Bushmills." The agent faked a greedy haul of whiskey and wiped his mouth with the back of his hand.

Clem gave Sean a thick envelope stuffed with tens and twenties. "Here. This is reward money and something extra from the Bureau. The bonus officially makes you a paid informant and you have some people to meet in Philadelphia tomorrow bright and early. I suggest you use some of that for some new smart, but conservative clothing. If you comport yourself well there, you'll be going to Washington for training and they'll fill your head with bullshit, half of which you'll forget, if you're any good. Welcome to your new life, mister… whatever your name is now."

Osmund said, "Get yourself ready for a drive. You'll ride with me so I can coach you about talking to our boss. He's a short guy with no neck who will have an unlit cigar in his hand, which he will point at you now and again for emphasis. When he finally lights the thing and blows a noxious cloud at you, the interview is over. He won't be the last guy you talk to, either. You will be on the grill all day but when I'm finished with you they'll all be your lap dogs."

"I'm your willing pupil, Ollie."

Agent Stanley took Eunice's coffee mug to the sink. When he turned back to Sean he said, "Eunice and I are counting on you to conduct yourself accordingly. It wouldn't do for you to make a bad impression and scotch my career before our wedding."

"Oh, congratulations to the both of you. Can I give the bride away?"

"Uh, no, since you're so dead and all."

21

PLACES WHERE ONLY ECHOES GO

S ean's life changed profoundly after his collision in the shadows behind the McFarland House with Merle Yates. In some ways he would continue to live as he did before that pivotal night. For one thing, he never really escaped the shadows. He still lied and took on roles and names that were far removed from who Sean Daugherty was. He had merely changed masters. His new masters were fond of meetings.

In Philadelphia, he was interviewed first by an entire panel of FBI agents who saw no risk in bringing him on board. The second round of inquiries was a professional courtesy to the Office of Strategic Services. Clem's boss had received a request. The vetting of operatives with the OSS required much more than the official reports from Clement Stanley's desk. He would have a third interview again with the FBI in D. C. When Sean boarded a train for Washington he knew the stakes were high. The two hours he spent in OSS headquarters seemed like twenty. He was warned by a man in uniform that things could get very ugly for him the instant there is any hint of disloyalty. "Remember, Sean you are already presumed dead so when you *are* dead, what's the difference?" Sean had no idea when he left Elk County that the things he had in his head were of such a premium value to so many people. Osmund's coaching had been invaluable when it came to dealing with the intense scrutiny of the two agencies. At least he had friends.

When he finished his OSS interview, Sean returned to FBI headquarters and sat in a large room with telephones, teletype machines and blackboards full of diagrams that meant nothing to him. Sean was unaware until that moment that Agent Stanley had come to D. C. too. Clem came in with a tray full of egg salad sandwiches and apple pie. The two ate their fill and sipped at lemonade. They talked about some of the better baseball pitchers and the best places in the East to drink beer and eat seafood. Clem made no mention of the phone call he had received very early that morning. The caller had an impressive title and he said his call was on behalf his division of the Office for Strategic Services. Lieutenant Colonel George Paxton (Clem chuckled at the pseudonym) made it immediately clear that he intended to meet with Sean Daugherty and that the meeting's purposes was not to gather intelligence. Paxton would prefer to have a crack at Mix Wizard himself. Paxton described his proposal in simple terms: If he liked what he saw, Sean would go to work for him. Sean's alternative was the United States Disciplinary Barracks in Leavenworth. There would be no trial.

Clem sat forward in his chair. It made a sudden screech. Without stopping to choose his words, he spat out his opinion of the Lieutenant Colonel's proposal.

"Now why would we just give you the prize turkey, Lieutenant?"

"Lieutenant Colonel."

"Okay. Tell me, why would I do that?"

"Oliver Osmund is a pretty fair fiction writer, Clem, but he's no Hemmingway. There are some gaps in his report I could drive a truck through. Filing a false report - that's serious. We have intelligence on your conduct in Elk County as well. That's what we do. You made some pretty serious errors in judgment, or at the very least some creative interpretations of protocol. Would you like me to go on?"

"I would like you to kiss my… Okay. You guys are good. You're really good. If I send you Sean and he doesn't care to be recruited, what happens?"

"I think he's going to take our deal. It won't be a good day for anyone if he doesn't."

The phone line was silent. The Lieutenant Colonel signed some papers and waited. Finally, Clem said, "When I think about it, he could do more with your resources than with ours. We will just red tape him to death. That's the reason I'm going along with this."

"Don't sell me, Clem. Sell Mister Daugherty."

"Consider it done. But it's not selling. He does it or he doesn't. His choice." This last pitch was pure baloney. Clem was trying to get the last word in but he was beginning to think about the consequences for Sean and Osmund and Eunice. How would Eunice enjoy marrying an unemployed man? He was going to have to get past Paxton's audacity and simply swallow this one.

The OSS officer said, "I didn't hear some of that. Just the part about my considering it done. That's very good Agent Stanley, very good. God bless the USA."

"And all the ships at sea." Clem hung up. He cancelled his appointments and headed for Pennsylvania Avenue. Just before loading the tray with lunch he asked an operator for direct line to the OSS office in Washington. A secretary picked up the call and asked, "Who would you like to speak to today?"

"Is Lieutenant Colonel George Paxton in, please?"

"No he is on his way to a meeting. Would you like to hold or call again later?"

"God bless the USA. No, that's fine, thanks."

After their lunch Clem choked up when he said goodbye. He knew that Sean was going into a very long, dark tunnel where he was likely to remain for many years. Under cover a man can confide in no one. The loneliness is deathly. He knew that Eunice would not be granted the privilege of a goodbye. That was exactly how it went.

*   *   *

Later that year when Sean's training was complete, he became Devon Heaney (his primary alias) who, during his tenure with the OSS and later the new Central Intelligence Agency, gathered evidence on thirteen major operatives from six different countries. Eleven of these operatives were jailed, recruited as double agents, or otherwise neutralized. The other two had accused one another of compromising their operation and Sean was wounded as he attempted to stop them from killing each other. That was his last assignment. He left the CIA grieving for that couple, a man and woman on the wrong side politically. Sean discovered that the two spies, were falsely accused of atrocities and after he had "befriended" them under cover he lost his professional distance. Their confusion and distrust of each other had been his doing. Their death was his undoing. It was the result that had been ordered to get. The lines between Sean and his subjects had become blurry. Like many others whom he was sent to destroy, they looked more like friends than enemies, more like people with lives and families and hearts and souls. The older Sean became, the less suited he was for his work. He awoke to a snowy sunrise one morning and somewhere in the drifts not far from his window he saw the end of his career.

Sean had begun his new life by ending the careers of the three saboteurs he was working with and his replacement bomb-maker, named by some cosmic coincidence, Elliot Thompson. The Elliot Company case was considered a triumph among decision makers in the FBI, the OSS and the Department of War. No lives were lost at the plant itself. More importantly, the world's most reliable and ultra-quiet submarine engines the company made in Ridgway saved the lives of many hundreds of navy men.

Sean was involved in many critical operations, not the least of which was a leadership role on a team that successfully sabotaged the German military's supply of heavy water. Devon Heaney's team of Milorg Norwegian resistance forces planted magnetic charges on the ferry, Hydro. The detonation was timed perfectly and the fertilizer barge sank in 1300 feet of water. The entire Nazi atomic bomb project was irreparably thwarted by this single explosion. Several boxcars full of heavy water, which had been loaded on the ferry, went to the bottom with it. The following day four of the train cars floated back to the surface but the damage was too severe for the project to make a recovery. The process of accumulation of this crucial ingredient was too slow to provide enough to arm a weapon before the war ended.

Sean never married because, he said, "I couldn't expect a woman to live the life I would give her."

Clement and Eunice and their children, Sean and Verna moved to Richmond, Virginia after the war. Eunice became the editor of a women's magazine and Clem opened a motorcycle shop.

Oliver Osmund died of prostate cancer in 1953. Devon Heaney and Clem Stanley organized a series of motorcycle races in the US and Canada to benefit the Osmund family fund. Osmund's wife and five children were well taken care of.

To everyone he had known in Elk County Sean remained dead and gone. He retired from public service in 1969, got a degree and became a high school chemistry teacher in Bangor Maine, the city where Hammond and Sharp had lived. His two-bedroom bungalow was two blocks from the boarding house where Merle Yates had reserved a room 28 years to the day before Sean signed his lease. In 1988 he retired from public school teaching to raise sheep, build furniture and keep bees on his farm twenty miles south of Bangor. Every Christmas the Stanley family receives a crate of honey and presents for the Stanley grandchildren. It comes from their honorary uncle Devon, whom they never met.

Sean's favorite memories of Bangor were of his many students. Each night he graded their work and afterword he would walk his dog, Gem Beag, past the former living space of the man who, as Clement Stanley's story said, killed Sean Daugherty.

ABOUT THE AUTHOR

Joe Bliskey grew up in Pennsylvania, where he spent his first twenty-one years on the edge of the Allegheny National Forest. He is a professional musician, lyricist and published poet who wrote a newspaper column for a time in his hometown weekly about music and film. He moved his family to Texas in 1980 where he took a job in high-tech industry and continued to play part time in local rock and country bands. His first two novels, *The Parent File* and *The Jonas File* will be published soon as a series. The former is a medical mystery and the latter is a humor piece about three boys who lived in Roswell, New Mexico in the 1970s.

To send the author a comment, email him at:
diffdrum14@gmail.com

Facebook Search Term: **Different Drum Books**